William Harrison Ainsworth

Hilary St. Ives

Vol. II

William Harrison Ainsworth

Hilary St. Ives
Vol. II

ISBN/EAN: 9783337040536

Printed in Europe, USA, Canada, Australia, Japan

Cover: Foto ©Andreas Hilbeck / pixelio.de

More available books at **www.hansebooks.com**

HILARY ST. IVES.

A Novel.

BY

WILLIAM HARRISON AINSWORTH.

IN THREE VOLUMES.

VOL. II.

LONDON:

CHAPMAN AND HALL, 193, PICCADILLY.

1870.

CONTENTS OF VOL. II.

BOOK II.

MYRTILLA.

Hilary St. Ives.

BOOK II.

MYRTILLA.

VOL. II.   B

I.

NOT every woman who can move about gracefully in a riding-habit. Lady Richborough understood the art to perfection, and never looked better, or seemed more at ease than when attired *en Amazone.* The costume was exactly adapted to her incomparable figure. And how becoming was the hat surmounting the chignon in which her rich black tresses were braided.

While pacing to and fro on the lawn, chatting merrily with Oswald, with the skirts of her habit

B 2

under her arm, and a little whip in her hand, her charming ladyship contrived to indulge her companion with a glimpse of a foot worthy of Cinderella, clad in the daintiest boot imaginable.

Sir Charles Ilminster was likewise upon the lawn, sauntering about by himself. He had by no means the confident air of a hopeful suitor. On the contrary, he looked thoughtful, and cast many an anxious glance towards the house, and when at last the object of his affections came forth, a tremor passed through his frame.

The joyous shout raised by Lady Richborough on sight of May, was blithely responded to by the fair young damsel. In another moment they had met, and embraced. The meeting was witnessed by Colonel Delacombe and Mr. Thornton, who had lingered behind on the terrace, and very much delighted they both were with the spectacle.

" Deuced fine woman, Lady Richborough !"
exclaimed the colonel. " Never saw a finer figure
in my life."

" Magnificent !" cried the old gentleman.

Mr. Radcliffe followed his daughter as quickly
as he could, and cordially greeted Sir Charles.
But it did not fare so well with the baronet, as
it had done with his sister. When he advanced
to pay his devoirs to May, he was coldly received—so much so as to attract the attention
of the spectators on the terrace. Not being in
the secret, the colonel attached little importance
to the circumstance, but Mr. Thornton was
greatly put out by it.

" Zounds !" he mentally ejaculated. " I suspect
the little hussy means to refuse him. Mustn't
be. Height of folly to throw away such a
chance."

He then proposed to the colonel that they

should join the party on the lawn, and proceeding thither, they were presented in due form to
Lady Richborough and Sir Charles. Her ladyship's charms lost nothing by nearer inspection—
rather gained. If the colonel was charmed with
her, she was not less struck by his distinguished
appearance and manner. But she had too much
tact to neglect Mr. Thornton, and quite captivated the old gentleman by the civil things she
said to him. How could he resist such honeyed
words from lips so rosy?

Colonel Delacombe got on very well with Sir
Charles. Habitually, as we have remarked, the
baronet was reserved and haughty, but he was
prepossessed by the colonel's manner, which was
unquestionably fascinating, and, besides, he knew
all about him. So they were speedily on very
friendly terms. Sir Charles had many friends in
India, with most of whom Colonel Delacombe

was acquainted, and could give him tidings of them. So well pleased was the baronet with his new acquaintance, that before they had been long together, he told him he should be delighted to see him at Boxgrove.

Overhearing the invitation, Lady Richborough warmly seconded it.

"I am sure you will be pleased with the old place," she said, with a look that was quite irresistible.

The colonel felt sure he should, and added that the invitation was a great deal too tempting to be refused.

Meantime, Mr. Thornton, who was resolved to have a word with his grand-daughter before any mischief was done, beckoned to her to follow him, and led her away from the company.

As soon as they were out of earshot, the old gentleman began without preamble.

"Your papa has intimated to me that you mean to refuse Sir Charles Ilminster. Now, my dear child, I tell you plainly you must do nothing of the sort. There cannot be two opinions as to the eligibility of Sir Charles. He is quite as good a match as you can ever expect to make. Your union with him will place you in an excellent social position, and will be satisfactory to us all, while it must be conducive to your own happiness.

"Don't interrupt me, I beg. I won't listen to any observations. I know the silly arguments you are about to employ. 'You can't make up your mind'—'you don't care for him,' and so forth. Stuff and nonsense! You cannot fail to like Sir Charles; and as to making up your mind, since you are incapable of deciding for yourself, we must decide for you."

"But I have decided, dear grandpapa—quite decided."

"Not in the right way. You have decided to refuse Sir Charles. I won't allow you to commit such folly."

"Really, grandpapa, you are very unreasonable. I have no desire to marry just at present."

"Humph! I know better. Every girl of nineteen wishes to be married, whatever she may aver to the contrary. But even if you do desire to remain single a little longer, it is your bounden duty to accede to the wishes of your family. Nothing, I repeat, can be more satisfactory to us than the proposed alliance; and I, for one, shall be wofully disappointed if it does not take place. Your papa and mamma have not spoken to you as strongly as they ought to have done. They have not put the matter in the right light. They are too indulgent by half, and I have told them so. You appear to entertain most erroneous notions in regard to matrimonial arrangements. A girl has no voice in them—or ought to have none. She must take the man chosen for her, whether she likes him or not. Do you mark that?"

"If you did not speak so seriously, grandpapa, I should think you were jesting."

" Parents expect implicit obedience to their will," pursued the old gentleman. "A girl's inclinations are rarely, if ever, consulted. Still more rarely is there any opposition on her part, because she knows that the best has been done for her. All important marriages are arranged on this plan. Mamma settles them. They may be styled ' Marriages of convenience.' What of that? They are far better than foolish love-matches that always end unhappily. Now, my dear child, I trust it won't be necessary for me to say more to ensure obedience to my injunctions. Put aside all nonsensical feeling, and accept Sir Charles."

" Anything in reason to please you, dear grand-papa," she rejoined. " But not this."

" You must—you *shall* accept him!" he cried, exasperated by her refusal.

The old gentleman had grown so terribly red in the face, that May feared he would have a fit of apoplexy, and it was a great relief to her when Lady Richborough and Oswald were seen ap-proaching.

Delighted to escape from a further lecture, she hastened to meet her ladyship.

" The gentlemen are gone to look at the plants in the greenhouses," observed Lady Richborough. " But I declined to accompany them, for I want to have a little talk with you, May. How exces-sively hot it is !"

" Suppose we sit down for a few minutes in the summer-house ?" said May. " You will find it cool there."

"A delightful suggestion. You will know where to find us if we are wanted," she remarked, with an arch look at Oswald.

"Mind what I have said to you, May," cried Mr. Thornton, as the two ladies tripped off.

"What has grandpapa been saying to you, my love?" inquired her ladyship.

"Giving me a lecture," replied the other. "He is a very positive old gentleman, and likes his own way."

"But very fond of you, I'm sure, so you ought to let him have it," observed Lady Richborough, who suspected the truth.

"Harkee, Oswald," cried Mr. Thornton to his grandson; "I have a question to ask you, and I expect a straightforward answer. Have you proposed to your fair cousin?"

Oswald stammered out something, but could not deny the soft impeachment.

"And been rejected, eh?"

Impossible to offer a contradiction.

"I thought as much. Your poor mother persuaded herself that the affair was in excellent train, and would be settled as soon as I made my appearance, but she seems to have been out in her calculations, or you have misled her. Never mind, my boy, never mind. You must look elsewhere for a wife. And you needn't look far," he observed, with a knowing wink—" not farther than Boxgrove."

"No chance there, sir," replied Oswald. "Lady Richborough is a monstrous fine woman, but above my mark."

" Poh! poh! you don't know whether you've a chance or not till you try. Were I in your place I wouldn't hesitate."

" But there's a difficulty to get over, sir, of which you may not be aware. Her ladyship forfeits her jointure if she marries again."

" S'death! that is awkward — confoundedly

awkward. I promised your mother I would do something handsome for you on your marriage, and so I will. But her highflying ladyship couldn't live on a paltry pittance of a thousand a year."

" I fear not, sir. Therefore I must give up all idea of such a match. Besides, to confess the truth, I can't get May out of my head."

"Think no more about her, I tell you. We have other designs for May. A little flirtation with her ladyship—if it comes to nothing—will cure you of your foolish passion. By-the-by, you haven't told me *why* May refused you. I thought she liked you, and so did your mother. Has she any other attachment?"

" None that I'm aware of, sir. I was fool enough to believe she liked me. She seems to have a sort of fancy for that young artist who has got into the house. A forward, presuming

fellow, who doesn't seem to know his proper position."

"Then he must be taught it," rejoined the
old gentleman. "But I can't believe May would
bestow a serious thought on *him.*"

"She was a good deal taken up with him this
morning, I can tell you, sir," observed Oswald,
whose jealousy had been aroused, as we know—
"more than I ever saw her with any one before."

"You don't say so!" exclaimed Mr. Thornton.
"Then the sooner we get rid of him the better."

"You'll find some difficulty with my aunt, I
fear, sir," said Oswald. "She has taken an
amazing fancy to the young fellow."

"Has she, by Jove!" cried the old gentleman,
stopping to reflect. "More than ever necessary
he should be got out of the house without delay.
I know who will help us to do it. For some
reason that I can't exactly understand," he added,

with a comical look, "Colonel Delacombe seems vexed at finding the young man here."

"No wonder," cried Oswald. "It must be a bore to meet with a fellow who might pass for one's son."

"A word from the colonel to your aunt will do the business," said the old gentleman, chuckling. "Mr. Hilary St. Ives shall soon bid adieu to Hazlemere—that I can promise him."

As they gained the terrace, they met the rest of the gentlemen coming out of the greenhouses, with which they seemed greatly pleased. Sir Charles was loud in his commendations of Macdonald, and said his own head-gardener might take a lesson from him.

As soon as he could find an opportunity, the old gentleman addressed himself to the colonel, and while he was opening his business to him, Sir Charles inquired of Oswald what had become of the ladies. On learning they were in the summer-house, he immediately set off by himself in that direction.

As yet, he had had no conversation with Mr. Radcliffe on the subject next his heart.

II.

IN THE SUMMER-HOUSE.

"WELL, my love," cried Lady Richborough, laying down her whip, and taking off her hat, as they entered the summer-house, "I have a great deal to say to you, but I scarcely know where to begin. However, I must dash into the thick of it, or I shall never get on. Of course you have seen Sir Charles's letter, but I can assure you it gives a very inadequate idea of the dear boy's feelings, for he is desperately smitten. I confess I don't approve of such a formal mode of proceeding. An offer comes best from a man's own lips, for then it springs straight from the heart, and there can be no mistake about it— but Charlie would have his own way. Ah! if I were to repeat all the rapturous things he has uttered about you, I should tire your patience as much as he has tired mine. Your name has been coupled with every endearing epithet in the language. Sixty times in the hour is it pronounced—that is, once in every minute."

"You are laughing at me," observed May.

"No such thing. I am trying to give you an idea of the dear boy's condition. I have known many a man who has been suffering from heart complaint, but I never knew a worse case than Charlie's. You must take pity on him, or you will be answerable for the fatal consequences certain to ensue."

"I should be sorry to be the cause of Sir

Charles's death," replied May, smiling. "But I have no apprehension of any such result."

"Neither have I," rejoined her ladyship, "Because I feel sure you will compassionate him. Come, now we are alone, confess that you do love him—a very little bit. I see you do—though you won't answer. The dear boy deserves your love, for though he is my brother, I will say that a better fellow does not exist. If he has a fault I have never been able to discover it. He is the most refined, sensitive creature possible. A woman must be an angel to come up to his ideal."

"But I am not an angel, dear Lady Richborough," observed May, laughing.

"You are in Charlie's eyes," rejoined her ladyship. "But call me Myrtilla—just as I call you May—for I now regard you as a sister. I must take some credit to myself for making the dear boy sensible of your merits. A hundred to one if he would have observed you, if I had not pointed you out, and given him my opinion about you. But on the very first interview those bright eyes did their business. Are you not vain of your conquest? You ought to be."

"Dearest Lady Richborough——"

"Myrtilla, my love, if you please."

"Well, dearest Myrtilla, I cannot allow you to go on in this strain. I need not say how much flattered I feel by Sir Charles's offer, but——"

"You don't mean to say you have the slightest idea of refusing him?" cried her ladyship, in astonishment. "Impossible! I have a better idea of your judgment."

"I really cannot make up my mind," said May, blushing and greatly embarrassed.

"Oh! if you're only undecided I don't care,"

cried Lady Richborough, laughing. "I really didn't expect to be called upon to plead the dear boy's suit, because I thought the advantages of the offer would be obvious."

"I have the highest opinion of Sir Charles in every respect," said May. "But I cannot give him my heart."

"Have you given it to any one else?" demanded her ladyship.

"No," replied May, firmly.

"Then you may safely accept him. Love will come hereafter."

"But would it be fair to Sir Charles to act thus?"

Lady Richborough was rather puzzled by the question, but she answered promptly,

"Yes, I do not think any man has a right to expect more. Sir Charles's character must command your respect—his devotion cannot fail to win your love. I counsel you to accept him."

At this critical juncture, and as if he had been expressly summoned, Sir Charles himself stood before them.

Smiling at her brother, Lady Richborough immediately arose, took up her hat and whip, and prepared to depart.

"Do not leave me, Myrtilla, I entreat," whispered May.

"Nay, my love, you must listen to the dear boy. A word from you will make him supremely happy. All's right," she whispered to Sir Charles, as she passed out. "Go in and win!"

III.

MRS. RADCLIFFE GIVES HILARY ADVICE.

Now to return to the boudoir.

After begging Hilary to be seated, Mrs. Radcliffe observed,

"I think I can guess what is passing in your breast, Mr. St. Ives. You fancy you have discovered some solution to the mystery of your birth. I should be sorry to excite hopes that may never be realised—at the same time I cannot altogether discourage you. I will frankly own that the interest I felt in you at first was caused by the remarkable likeness you bear to Colonel Delacombe. There is a miniature of the colonel—taken when young. It might pass for your portrait."

"Astonishing!" exclaimed Hilary, gazing at the miniature. "I am fairly bewildered."

"I am a good deal perplexed myself," pursued Mrs. Radcliffe; "but one thing seems tolerably clear. Although the colonel feigned surprise on seeing you just now, I am pretty certain he knew you were here. I will tell you why I think so. This morning, I understand, you have received five hundred pounds from an unknown friend?"

"Very true."

"You have also received a chest containing a large supply of wearing apparel and other things. Who could have sent the money and the chest?"

"No one but Colonel Delacombe!" exclaimed Hilary, eagerly.

"The colonel has only just returned from India," said Mrs. Radcliffe. "His first inquiries have evidently been about you. Having ascertained that you are here—though how he obtained the information I cannot explain—his immediate impulse was to send you assistance. His next was to run down and see you, which he persuaded himself he could do with safety. But the likeness between you—of which I suppose he was ignorant—has betrayed him."

"You have divined it all," cried Hilary.

Mrs. Radcliffe smiled at this tribute to her perspicacity.

"Of course he pretends that his visit is paid to me, but I know better," she said. "I am not to be duped by such a shallow artifice. He has come to see *you*, and satisfy himself, by

personal inspection, what you are like. That is
his object, I am convinced."

" I am lost in wonder at your penetration,
madam," exclaimed Hilary. "Nothing seems to
have escaped you."

" Another point of the last importance has
yet to be mentioned," pursued Mrs. Radcliffe.
" The arms engraved upon the signet-ring which
you wear are the colonel's."

" Great heavens! is it possible? I have always
been told that this ring was my father's?"

Mrs. Radcliffe smiled and nodded her head.

" I must beg you to entrust that ring to me
for a time, for reasons which I will presently
explain. It will be perfectly safe with me, I
can assure you."

He gave it to her at once, and she locked
it up in a drawer of the table.

" I do not wish the colonel to see it at

present," she said ; " and he could not fail to
do so, if you continue to wear it. And now I
must give you a few hints as to the course I
think you ought to pursue. We will suppose
our notions to be correct. Clearly, the first thing
you have to do is to ingratiate yourself with the
colonel. To succeed in this object will require
care on your part. Do not seem too curious.
Do not annoy him with any more questions.
Evidently, as I have explained, he came here to
reconnoitre. Let him take his own time, and
proceed in his own way. Do not presume in the
slightest degree on the discovery which you believe you have made. Do not allude to the
likeness that seems to proclaim your parentage.
By proper management, you may perhaps in the
end induce him to acknowledge you. But this
desirable consummation can only be brought about
by prudence and caution. Like every one else,

the colonel has his peculiarities, and in order to win his favour they must be studied."

"I hope to make him proud to acknowledge me," cried Hilary.

"Precisely what I would have you do, and I therefore urge you not to precipitate matters."

"I see the policy of the course you suggest, madam," said Hilary, with a look of inexpressible gratitude, "and will strive to follow it most carefully."

"I will give you all the aid I can," said Mrs. Radcliffe. "And now another word of caution. You will be surprised when I counsel you not to take Mrs. Sutton into your confidence. She is the best creature living, and I have every faith in her. But from some cause or other—I know not what—she has conceived a strong dislike to Colonel Delacombe, and may thwart your plans."

"I will not neglect your counsel, madam," said the young man. "But I could have trusted Mrs. Sutton with my life."

"Do not trust her now."

After a little pause she said:

"That you may fully comprehend the almost maternal interest I take in you, I must let you into a secret. Seymour Delacombe—I mean the colonel, of course—was my first love. I was engaged to him; but the engagement was broken off, and I was married to Mr. Radcliffe. Now you will understand what strange emotions were roused in my breast when I beheld one who so strongly resembled Seymour. Yes," she continued, carried away by excitement, and almost heedless what she said, "I thought what might have been, had fate permitted, and for the moment looked upon you as a son!"

Hilary started to his feet, doubting whether he had heard aright.

But another person—the very last who ought
to have done so—heard the words. This was the
lady's husband, who chanced to enter the boudoir
at the moment.

However, we hasten to say that he attached
very little importance at the time to the expres-
sions, though he afterwards recalled them.

IV.

THE SCHEME FRUSTRATED.

SEEING he was in the way, and a good deal confused, Hilary prepared to quit the room. Just as he was going out, Mrs. Radcliffe told him she would come down stairs presently, and introduce him to Sir Charles and his sister.

"My dear," said Mr. Radcliffe, as soon as they were alone, " you have promised more than you are likely to perform."

" Why so?" she inquired.

" I do not think it would be agreeable to

Colonel Delacombe that this young man should be introduced to our friends. In fact, as things have turned out, it is rather unlucky that he happens to be here at this juncture; and I think the best plan will be to get rid of him—civilly, of course—as soon as we can."

"The thing is impossible, my dear," said his wife; "I have asked him to stay."

"Yes, but we must make some excuse. I see no harm in the young fellow—none whatever— and am quite willing that he should remain— indeed, I am sorry to send him away—but to tell you the truth, your father objects very strongly to him."

Mr. Radcliffe thought this argument would be unanswerable, but he was mistaken.

"Neither to please the colonel, nor to please papa, nor to please you, sir, can I allow Mr. St. Ives to go," said the lady, decidedly.

"I wish you could induce him to keep his own room then," groaned Mr. Radcliffe. "At any rate, let me beg of you not to introduce him to Lady Richborough and Sir Charles, or you will place me in a very awkward position."

"I cannot see why you should be uneasy," remarked the lady. "Mr. St. Ives is very gentlemanlike, and our friends will understand that he is an artist."

"But he will make the colonel look ridiculous, my dear. Can you understand that?"

"No, I confess I don't see it," said the lady.

Very opportunely the colonel and Mr. Thornton here entered the boudoir.

Thus strongly reinforced, Mr. Radcliffe ventured to renew the attack.

"I've been telling my wife, colonel, that you object to this young spark—this Hilary St. Ives," he said.

"I refuse to believe so unless I have it from your own lips, colonel," observed the lady, with one of her blandest smiles. "You have seen nothing of him."

"I have seen quite enough," rejoined the colonel. "I have no personal objection to the young fellow, and I regret to eject him from such comfortable quarters, but upon my soul! I think the joke has been carried far enough. I can't stand more of it."

"No joke is intended, my dear colonel. Surely, you don't suppose so?"

"Everybody else will think so, if I don't," he rejoined.

"I object to the fellow on other grounds," interposed Mr. Thornton. "A conceited puppy —and if I didn't fear offending the colonel I should say he presumes upon his likeness to him."

"How extremely silly you are, papa. The colonel will laugh at you."

"My dear lady," said the colonel, "I should not care about the matter if it were confined to your own circle—you are welcome to laugh at me as much as you please. But I cannot be made ridiculous in the eyes of Lady Richborough and Sir Charles."

"Didn't I say so, my dear?" cried Mr. Radcliffe.

"What would you have me do?" said the lady, with an imploring look at the colonel, which she thought would move him. "I have asked Mr. St. Ives to stay. I did not think his presence would be disagreeable to you."

"But it *is* disagreeable to him," cried Mr. Thornton — "infernally disagreeable. It is disagreeable also to me."

Mr. Radcliffe did not venture to make a remark.

"It comes to this, my dear Mrs. Radcliffe," said

the colonel, "that either he or I must go. Make your choice."

"Nay, then, I cannot hesitate," said the lady; "though I yield very much against my inclination."

"I'll go and give the young fellow his congé," cried Mr. Thornton, chuckling at the notion.

"Spare his feelings, I entreat, papa," said Mrs Radcliffe.

"Oh yes, I'll spare him."

"I must see him before he leaves—tell him so."

"Of course, he'll come to bid you good-by."

The old gentleman winked at Mr. Radcliffe, and they left the room together.

"I think you will be sorry for compelling me to take this step, Seymour," observed the lady, in a tone of reproach, as soon as they were alone. "Have you no interest in this young man?"

"Interest!—none," he replied.

She shook her head sceptically.

"You cannot deceive me. You have defeated a scheme which I had devised for his benefit."

"It is not too late to repair the error," said the colonel. "If you have any motive for detaining him I will take my departure."

"My motive was to serve you, Seymour," said the lady.

"Serve me! I really cannot understand all these innuendoes."

Mrs. Radcliffe was about to reply, when the door opened, and Hilary entered the boudoir. His looks showed that he was greatly hurt and offended.

"After what passed between us a short time ago, madam," he said, "and the interest you professed to take in me, I did not expect to be thus summarily dismissed. It is to you, sir, I presume that I owe my dismissal?" he added to the colonel.

You are welcome to entertain any opinion you please, sir," rejoined the other, haughtily.

"For Heaven's sake, Seymour," cried the lady, " do not treat him thus."

Hilary, who was evidently struggling with violently repressed emotion, said, in a hoarse voice, to Mrs. Radcliffe,

" May I speak to him ?"

" No, no," she replied ; " not now."

" I am de trop here, I perceive," said the colonel. " I have the honour to wish you good day, Mr. St. Ives."

" A moment, sir !" cried the young man, trying to detain him.

But the colonel repulsed him with a haughty gesture, and went out.

Hilary's enfeebled state did not enable him to bear up longer. He sank on the sofa, and Mrs. Radcliffe, alarmed by his looks, rang the bell.

As the colonel issued forth into the passage he found Mrs. Sutton. She had evidently heard what had just passed in the boudoir. Seizing his arm, and fixing a threatening look upon him, she said,

"I told you you ought not have come here. You have broken the compact, and are interfering with me. If this young man is driven away, look to yourself."

"I have made no compact with you, woman. Do as you please," rejoined the colonel. And disengaging himself from her, strode on.

Just then the bell sounded, and Mrs. Sutton entered the boudoir.

On seeing Hilary's condition, she cast an angry and reproachful look at her mistress, that seemed to imply, "This is your work."

"I could not help it," cried Mrs. Radcliffe. "Don't upbraid me—but assist him."

Fortunately, there were plenty of restoratives

at hand, and some of these being applied by
the housekeeper, the young man soon regained
his consciousness.

But he looked ghastly pale, and was still very
feeble. He made an effort to rise, but fell back
again.

"I cannot tell what has come over me," he
murmured, trying to force a smile.

"The agitation you have just undergone has
been too much for you," said Mrs. Radcliffe.
"You must not think of leaving to-day. What
say you, Sutton?" she added, appealing to her.

"You are the best judge," replied the housekeeper, coldly. "In my opinion he is not in a
fit state to move. He ought not to have left his
room at all to-day. Had he remained quiet this
would not have happened. Worse may ensue.
If he leaves the house, I will not answer for his
life."

"He shall not go," said Mrs. Radcliffe, alarmed.

"Pray do not give yourself any further concern about me," said Hilary. "There is no real danger, I am sure. This faintness will soon pass. I cannot remain here longer."

"Not if I command you?" rejoined Mrs. Radcliffe. "Have I not just said that I feel towards you as a mother?" she added, in a low, tender tone. "Stay for my sake. Mrs. Sutton cannot feel for you as I do, but she will take every care of you."

"*I* cannot feel for him!" exclaimed the housekeeper, with a burst of uncontrollable rage. "Oh, this is too much!"

"Forgive me, Sutton," said Mrs. Radcliffe, frightened. "You have done all that could be done for him—far more than I could have done. But—you understand."

"Yes, yes, I understand," rejoined the housekeeper.

"Are you able to move now, do you think?"
she added to the young man, who arose with her
assistance.

"Oh yes, my strength is returning."

"Ah! that is well," cried Mrs. Radcliffe.
"Take him to his own room at once, Sutton.
I will come to see you presently," she added, in
her sweetest voice, to Hilary. "But keep quiet,
I beg of you, and on no account leave your own
room."

The young man promised compliance, and, with
a look that bespoke profound gratitude mingled
with almost filial affection, quitted the boudoir,
supported by the housekeeper.

Mrs. Radcliffe stood at the door, and watched
them as they moved slowly along the passage.

Just as they were about to enter a chamber
on the left, Hilary perceived her, and smiled
gratefully.

"He shall not leave, if I can prevent it," thought Mrs. Radcliffe, as she returned to the boudoir. "But I really must not neglect our guests," she added, adjusting her toilette, preparatory to going down-stairs.

V.

CONTRARY TO EXPECTATION, SIR CHARLES IS ACCEPTED.

Soon after leaving the summer-house, Lady Richborough encountered Oswald, who was coming in that direction. He told her he was looking for her ladyship and May.

"Turn back with me, Mr. Woodcot," she rejoined with an arch look. "May is in the summer-house with Sir Charles."

"With Sir Charles!" echoed Oswald.

"Yes, and I don't think they would care for your company. You must make up your mind to lose your fair cousin. Sir Charles is resolved to carry her off."

"Ah! this is the plan they have had in view," thought Oswald. "No wonder I have been sent to the right-about."

"You can't suppose I am so blind as not to have perceived that you are desperately enamoured of your fair cousin," pursued her ladyship, "and I wouldn't have allowed Sir Charles to interfere, if I hadn't found out that May doesn't requite your passion."

"Much obliged for your kind intentions in my behalf," rejoined Oswald. "Luckily, they are quite unnecessary, since your ladyship has already made me perfectly indifferent to any rivalry on the part of Sir Charles."

"Ah! indeed — you surprise me. I am very happy to learn that. The object has been achieved quite unconsciously, I assure you."

" Not quite unconsciously, I should think," ventured Oswald.

" I should like to know how I have done it?" she remarked.

" The explanation is easy enough, and yet I have scarcely the courage to make it. When I fell in love with May, I had not seen your lady-ship."

" Very prettily turned, upon my word, Mr. Woodcot," said her ladyship. " I am immensely flattered by being preferred to your charming cousin, but I cannot compliment you on your taste."

" It seems to me that I have given the best proof possible of taste," rejoined Oswald, " though I may be fairly taxed with inconstancy."

" Good again. You improve, Mr. Woodcot."

" I am glad to hear your ladyship say so," re-joined Oswald, rather more diffidently. " I am afraid I shall sink in your esteem if I venture to describe the effect produced upon me by your charms."

Her ladyship did not seem at all displeased. She had flirted a good deal with Oswald on the previous day, when he had luncheoned at Boxgrove.

"Let us hear the state of the case," she observed, laughing. "Are you very hard hit?"

"Very hard," replied Oswald.

"What are your symptoms?" she inquired, with an arch look.

"Violent palpitations of the heart — troubled dreams—total loss of appetite—disordered brain—suicidal tendency."

"A very bad case indeed," she rejoined. "Shall I prescribe for you?"

"It rests with your ladyship to save my life," he cried, with an impassioned look. "I am entirely in your hands."

"Promise to attend to the prescription, or I cannot give it," she said.

Promise given.

"Drink an extra bottle of bordeaux to-day in honour of your fair cousin. To-morrow run up to town for a week, and before you come back you will have forgotten all about me. Your cure will then be complete."

While rattling on in this way, her ladyship had kept a watchful eye upon the summer-house. She now perceived the pair come forth, and, laughing heartily at Oswald's consternation, flew to meet them.

She augured well from her brother's looks.

"It's all right—I see it is!" she cried, seizing both May's hands. "Make me happy by saying you have put the dear boy out of his misery."

"I don't know what I have said," replied May, who looked pale and confused.

"Not at all surprising, my love. Girls never do know what they say on these occasions. They leave men to put their own construction on their words. How do you interpret her answer, Charlie?"

"Most favourably," he replied. "I have reason to believe I am accepted."

"Reason to believe, dear boy! That's not enough. You must be certain."

"I have asked for a few hours' consideration," observed May.

"But I hope Charlie has not been foolish enough to grant the request. Why keep the dear boy in suspense? I would not allow a moment's delay. It should be now or never with me. Let me give this little hand to Charlie, and conclude the matter."

May tried to withdraw her hand, but she could not prevent Sir Charles from pressing it to his lips.

Before a word of protest could be uttered, Lady

Richborough told May, in an undertone, that she could not now retract, and such was her ladyship's ascendancy over the young damsel that she felt unable to remonstrate.

" All is now satisfactorily concluded," cried her ladyship, greatly elated by her successful management. " I offer you both my heartfelt congratulations — you, my dear Charlie—and you, sweet sister that-is-to-be. May you both be as happy as I would have you !"

Just then the gong sounded for luncheon.

They were preparing to obey the summons, when Oswald, who had witnessed the scene at a distance—with what feelings we shall not attempt to describe—advanced towards them.

Lady Richborough begged him to go before them, and announce to Mr. and Mrs. Radcliffe that an engagement had just been concluded between May and Sir Charles.

"I am sure you will be delighted to be the bearer of the joyful intelligence," said her ladyship.

Oswald winced, but could not refuse, and, with a sore heart, departed on his mission.

The others followed more slowly to the house.

VI.

HILARY LEAVES HAZLEMERE.

IMAGINE papa's and mamma's amazement — imagine grandpapa's delight — when Oswald informed them that May had accepted Sir Charles.

"Many a girl, I know, has accepted the man she meant to refuse," observed papa; "but I didn't think May was one of that sort."

"Nor I," rejoined mamma, who had just come down-stairs, and was greeted by the intelligence. "I can't understand it."

"But I can," cried grandpapa, chuckling and

rubbing his hands gleefully. "It's all my doing. I've brought her to her senses."

"Begging your pardon, sir," remarked Oswald, "I should say, if May has been influenced by anybody, it is by Lady Richborough."

"Nothing of the sort," rejoined the old gentleman, sharply. "It's my doing, I tell you."

The foregoing discourse took place in the hall, where the party were assembled preparatory to going into the dining-room to luncheon. In another minute the newly-engaged couple came in, accompanied by Lady Richborough, who seemed in tip-top spirits. A scene of congratulations ensued, which will be readily conceived. While affectionately embracing his grand-daughter, the old gentleman whispered in her ear,

"You are a dear good girl, May, and won't regret following grandpapa's advice."

She made no reply. Indeed, she was almost

overcome, and her great desire was to be alone.
Rejoiced as he was at the resolution she had
taken, her father looked at her anxiously, and
noticed—not without misgiving—that she was
exceedingly pale. She did not go in to luncheon
with the others, but excusing herself to Lady
Richborough, hurried to her own room, and
throwing herself into a chair, gave vent to her
emotion in a flood of tears.

When she looked up, she perceived the housekeeper standing before her.

"Oh, Sutton!" she exclaimed, "I have been
very foolish—I have accepted him."

"I guessed as much," said the housekeeper,
coldly. "Well, I congratulate you."

"Pity me, rather."

"Pity you!" cried the housekeeper, contemp-
tuously. "No, I can't do that. Having taken
the step, you must abide by it. I believe you

have chosen well. You know my opinion of Sir Charles. Why are you not with them at luncheon ?"

" I could not stand it. I am going down presently. Where is Mr. St. Ives? I did not see him in the hall when I came in. I was glad he was not there."

Mrs. Sutton looked at her searchingly, as she replied,

"I do not think you will see him again. He has been enjoined to leave the house immediately."

"Enjoined to leave!" exclaimed May, indignantly. " By whom ?"

"By your grandpapa, but I believe at the instance of Colonel Delacombe. I am very sorry for it. But it cannot be helped."

"It must be prevented," cried May. " I will speak to grandpapa. He will not disoblige me so much. What does mamma say? Surely she will never allow Mr. St. Ives to be sent away thus!"

"What can she say, when every one is against her—even your papa? However, there is no use in discussing the matter. Mr. St. Ives is much hurt at the treatment he has experienced, and would not remain, even if requested. Unfortunately, he is scarcely in a fit state to move, for he has had a relapse, brought on by this excitement."

"Don't let him go, Sutton."

"I cannot prevent him, dear."

"I wish I could talk to him, but that would not be proper."

"I will tell him what you say," rejoined the housekeeper. "If it produces no other effect, it will console him."

And she departed on the errand.

Shortly afterwards, May left her room with the intention of joining the party at luncheon

In the passage, near the landing, she found Hilary and Mrs. Sutton. Evidently they were waiting for her coming forth. The young man moved forward feebly to meet her.

"I am come to bid you farewell, Miss Radcliffe," he said. "You have heard why I am leaving thus suddenly. I shall carry away with me a grateful recollection of your kindness."

"I have been urging him to delay his departure, but without effect," observed Mrs. Sutton.

"To remain longer would be impossible, after what has occurred," observed Hilary, in a tone that showed his resolution was taken.

"Farewell, then, since it must be so," rejoined May. "It will delight me to hear of your success."

"I shall strive to obtain distinction," he returned, "though I have not the incitement that I had to work. I have just heard that you are

to be united to Sir Charles Ilminster. May I
be allowed to wish you all possible happiness!"

Thanking him by a look, May again bade him
adieu, and went down-stairs.

With a deep sigh that seemed to proceed from
the inmost recesses of his breast, Hilary returned
to his room.

Mrs. Sutton did not go with him, her presence
being required below.

Hilary thought his heart would burst. All the
hopes in which he had so foolishly indulged were
crushed. The future was a blank. Worst of all,
he was stung well-nigh to madness by a sense of
wrong and injustice.

From this state he was roused by the entrance
of Boston, who brought him some sandwiches and
wine on a tray, which he placed on a little table
beside him.

"Sorry to find you've had another attack, sir,"

observed the valet, in a commiserating tone. "A glass of sherry, I'm sure, will do you good. Allow me to pour one out for you. We've just been drinking our young lady's good health in the servants' hall, and coupling with it the name of the honoured gentleman with whom she is to be united. Ah! sir, Sir Charles is a fortunate man, and could not have made a better choice."

"I trust she will be happy with him," said Hilary, raising the glass to his lips.

"Little doubt of it," cried Boston. "She'll have everything she can desire — a splendid mansion and a wealthy spouse. Boxgrove is the finest place in this part of Surrey. You've not seen Sir Charles, I think?—a noble-looking gentleman. And as to the love he bears our young lady, his groom, Kennedy, who has been dining with us in the servants' hall, told Annette that he's awful spoony. We shall all be sorry to lose Miss May— for she's the life and soul of the house—but we couldn't wish her a better home, or a better husband than she's sure to get."

Hilary assented in a scarcely audible voice.

"Everybody seems delighted with the engagement, except Mr. Oswald, and he looks rather down in the mouth—but that's not to be wondered at. I never saw master in greater glee than he was at luncheon, and as to Mr. Thornton, he's almost beside hisself. They're all going over to Boxgrove this afternoon, as Sir Charles wishes to show the place to Colonel Delacombe and the old gentleman. Pity you're not able to join the party, sir."

Hilary made no reply, and the valet, noticing his increased paleness, kindly urged him to take another glass of sherry, and try to eat a mouthful —but the young man declined.

"Is Mrs. Radcliffe going to Boxgrove?" he inquired.

"Yes, sir; and her ladyship has asked Mrs.

Sutton to accompany my mistress; so she's going too. The carriage is ordered immediately. That reminds me that I may be wanted. Can I do anything more for you, sir?"

"Nothing whatever," replied Hilary.

And the valet departed.

Shortly afterwards, Mrs. Radcliffe and the housekeeper entered the room—both arrayed for the drive. Mrs. Radcliffe was got up with great taste, and looked extremely well.

"I want to have some conversation with you," she said to the young man; "but I haven't time for it now. We're all going to Boxgrove, and shan't be back before seven o'clock in time for dinner. You'll have all the house to yourself, so ramble about it as you please, and do what you like. I can't stay a minute longer. Au revoir!"

Mrs. Sutton lingered for a moment, and said,

in a low voice, " I am obliged to go with her. Do nothing till my return."

She then followed her mistress out of the room.

All this occurred so quickly, that Hilary had not had time to speak, but feeling that some explanation of his intentions was due to Mrs. Radcliffe, he arose as quickly as he could, and went out into the passage. Too late. They were gone.

Merry voices mingled with laughter, resounding from the great staircase and from the entrance-hall, told him that the party were just starting on the expedition, and though he felt the sight would give him pain, he could not resist the impulse that prompted him to proceed to a window which he knew commanded the principal entrance of the house.

A well-appointed landau, to which a pair of splendid bays were harnessed, was drawn up at the

door. This carriage was destined for the elderly
parties—though Mrs. Radcliffe would not have
liked to be included in that list—and, as soon
as they were seated, it was driven off.

The saddle-horses were then brought round, and
the first to mount were Lady Richborough and
May. Though dazzled by her ladyship's beauty,
Hilary was far more attracted by May, whose
slight symmetrical figure was seen to great advantage in a riding-dress. If not so bold a rider as
her ladyship, May sat her steed with equal grace,
and looked more feminine—a special charm in
Hilary's eyes. Sir Charles was now privileged
to assist her to mount, and having performed this
enviable office, he sprang into his saddle, and they
rode off together. What would poor Hilary have
given to be by her side. He watched them as
they proceeded slowly towards the lodge-gates. It
was an aggravation of his misery to perceive that

May's lovely countenance had lost all trace of sad-
ness. She smiled complacently upon Sir Charles,
whose proud features wore an almost exulting expression.

Never, indeed, had the haughty baronet been
happier than at that moment. The prize was
won, when he had feared it would elude his grasp.

They were followed at a discreet distance by
Lady Richborough, escorted by Colonel Delacombe and Oswald. The colonel was provided
with the best hack in Mr. Radcliffe's stables—a
thoroughbred chesnut. Not knowing his rider,
the horse began to show off. But better horse-
man than Colonel Delacombe never existed, and
the skill with which he managed the fiery animal
filled Hilary with admiration. Even Lady Richborough was struck by the colonel's horsemanship,
and complimented him upon it. He smiled.
Praise from her ladyship was praise indeed.

From that moment she resolved upon his conquest, and set about the task in earnest. Oswald was not badly mounted, and looked well enough, but she did not bestow a thought upon him.

Hilary watched them, and listened to their laughter, till they had disappeared, and the sound of their voices could be heard no more.

With a sad heart he then returned to his chamber, and surrendered himself once more to bitter reflections.

He had taken leave of May for ever. She would soon be the bride of another. He must think of her no more. This was the sharpest pang.

Next in point of intensity was the anguish caused by Colonel Delacombe's treatment of him. Here, however, pride and indignation came to his relief, and allayed his mental torture.

The necessity for action aroused him. Writing materials were upon the table, and taking a sheet or two of paper he commenced a lengthened letter, the composition of which occupied him more than an hour, for he paused frequently while engaged in the task.

He did not dare to read over what he had written, but folding up the sheets, both of which he had filled, he placed within them the bank-notes he had received that morning, and securing the letter and inclosure in an envelope, addressed it to Mrs. Radcliffe.

Next unlocking the chest of clothes, which had been placed in a corner of the room, and taking from it a knapsack, sent him in lieu of the one of which he had been plundered, he packed up within it a couple of shirts, and a few other necessary articles. These and a round felt hat were all he took. His preparations being completed, he left the room, taking the letter with him.

On the landing of the staircase he encountered
Annette, to whom he confided the letter, request-
ing her to lay it on the table in her mistress's
boudoir.

Annette looked very much surprised, and noticing the knapsack, ventured to inquire if he
was about to take his departure.

Hilary replied in the affirmative, and putting
a small gratuity into her hand, bade her good-bye,
and descended the staircase. No one was in the
hall at the time, and he left the house without
attracting further observation.

Astonished at his abrupt departure, Annette did
his bidding, and took the letter to the boudoir,
twisting it about as she went, and wondering what
it contained.

VII.

BOXGROVE.

THE landau was slowly ascending the lofty and well-wooded hill on the summit of which stands the ancient mansion of the Ilminsters, when May and Sir Charles entered the park.

It was not May's first visit to Boxgrove. She had often been there before. But somehow the place looked different now — brighter and more cheerful. While cantering over the smooth turf, with Sir Charles by her side, gazing at her with admiration, she thought she had never discerned half the beauties of the park before. Perhaps the brilliant sunshine, flooding the groves and glittering on the vanes, gables, and bay-windows of the stately old pile, heightened the attraction of the prospect. A fine day will do wonders. But was there not something at work within her gentle breast? Was she not slightly elated by the idea that this proud domain might soon be hers? Certainly, as her eye ranged over the lovely scene, the thought crossed her, and quickened her pulse.

Boxgrove Park boasts timber of great age and great variety, wide-spread beeches, Druid oaks with huge gnarled trunks, Spanish chesnuts, and walnuts. No such walnuts to be found elsewhere. Besides these, there are hollies in abundance and of great size, splendid ilexes, groves of box that clothe the steepest parts of the hill, sombre avenues formed by black and matted yew-trees, while rows of tall straight pines edge

the paths that lead through the tangled thickets.
Here the red squirrel may be seen, here the
harsh jay may be heard, and many another
bird besides. In short, Boxgrove Park is very
beautiful, and very picturesque, and so May
thought it.

But what chiefly delighted her was a large
herd of deer couched beneath the trees about
a hundred yards from the spot where she had
halted for a moment to gaze around. Alarmed
by the notice taken of them, the graceful animals
quickly arose, and trooped off to an adjacent
covert. May watched their movements with the
greatest interest, and loudly expressed her admiration.

"Oh, the lovely creatures!" she exclaimed,
"how well they harmonise with the scene! No
park can be complete without deer."

"That is quite my opinion," observed Sir

Charles. "They are generally to be seen from the house, and form a very pretty picture. I hope you will take them under your especial charge."

May thanked him with a smile.

"By-and-by they will know me," she said, "and I shall not frighten them when stopping to look at them."

Nothing could have delighted Sir Charles more than this simple observation.

"I know you sketch," he said. "You will find plenty of exercise for your pencil here."

"Yes," she rejoined, "I have already noted one or two charming little bits that will exactly suit me. I could spend hours among those trees."

"I hope you will," he said; "and I hope I shall be near you."

"That will never do. I must be alone, or I shall not be able to sketch. I am an enthusiastic

admirer of old trees. Yonder aged oak is perfection. What a grand looking tree!"

" You have picked out the best tree in the
park," said Sir Charles. "That oak is called
'The King of the Forest,' and is older by some
centuries than the oldest tree near it. There are
some magnificent beech-trees on the north side
of the hill behind the house that deserve your
attention."

"I know them well," she rejoined. "They
are perfect beauties; such broad branches, and
such clean silvery stems. I have sketched one or
two of those beech-trees. Before long, I dare
say I shall have made acquaintance with every
tree in the park."

" Every tree in the park is yours from this
moment," he cried.

"A princely gift!" she exclaimed. "But
though I dote upon trees, I cannot accept it."

"Why not?" he demanded. "All I have is

yours. Having given you my heart, the rest goes with it."

Sir Charles looked so like a preux chevalier while making this gallant speech that May thought him superb. Homage like this is rarely paid now-a-days, and for the best of reasons—the girl of the period would laugh at it. With her the days of chivalry are for ever past. She does not understand the sentiment of devotion. Sentiment of any kind she derides. She neither desires to inspire a great passion, nor is capable of inspiring it. We have utterly failed in our portraiture of May, if she seems to bear any resemblance to a girl of this class. Hitherto, as we have shown, she cared very little for Sir Charles. She accepted him without knowing exactly why she did so—partly because she had been told most emphatically that her union with him would be agreeable to her family—but chiefly because she

yielded to the influence exercised over her by
Lady Richborough. Blame her not too severely,
fair censor. Very likely you would have acted
in the same way, if subjected to a similar ordeal.
The really surprising thing is, that she did not
fall in love with Sir Charles from the first. But
there is no accounting for tastes. After ac-
cepting him, she repented—but it was then too
late. During the ride to Boxgrove he made
wonderful progress in her regard. She listened
to what he said with pleasure — with something
more than pleasure. Love was fluttering around
her with his golden wings, though she could not
distinguish him. At the critical moment he let
fly the dart. Touched by Sir Charles's devotion,
she now felt for the first time that she could
love him. The thoughts passing in her breast
could be read in her looks, and Sir Charles was
not mistaken in them.

They were both roused from the delicious reverie, into which they had fallen, by light laughter, and looking round, beheld Lady Richborough approaching with her attendant cavaliers.

For the first time Sir Charles wished his sister away. In his present mood her high spirits were too much for him. As soon, therefore, as she and her companions came up, he said he should ride on to receive Mrs. Radcliffe, and with a look that conveyed a world of passionate regard to May, put spurs to his steed and galloped off towards the house. As he plunged into a grove of trees that lay between him and the mansion, May thought he looked like a paladin of old.

Reared about the middle of the sixteenth century by Sir Alberic Ilminster, Boxgrove was a magnificent mansion, partially castellated, with large transom windows filled with stained glass, and possessing many noble rooms, which were fortunately allowed to remain in their pristine state.

No material change had been made in the mansion since its erection, and even the old furniture, chairs, beds, antique mirrors, and hangings were carefully preserved, so that it was not merely a capital specimen of Tudor architecture, but gave an accurate idea of the internal decorations of a large house of the period.

The mansion was approached from the back through a turreted and embattled gateway, and over the entrance was a great stone shield, sculptured with the arms of the family. These were repeated on the garden gates, on the sundial, on the posts of the great staircase, on the huge chimney-piece of the hall, and were, furthermore, emblazoned on several of the windows.

The hall to which we have just adverted, and

which was entirely undefaced by modern altera-
tion, with its gallery for minstrels, its long mas-
sive oak table, its great fireplace and andirons,
recalled the days of baronial hospitality, which
Sir Alberic and many of his successors had practised. In the hall was a full-length portrait of
the doughty old knight, in ruff, doublet, and hose,
with his favourite black hound by his side, and
a certain resemblance might be traced in his
proud features to those of his descendant.

The drawing-room was splendid, the ceiling
being covered with a profusion of plaister orna-
ments, the wainscoting richly carved, and the
chimney-piece ornamented with pillars and terms,
and decorated with the arms of Elizabeth.

The dining-room had also a superb chimney-
piece and richly-carved wainscot.

At the head of the staircase was a grand
gallery, upwards of a hundred feet in length,

filled with family portraits. Hence a passage led
to the state bed-chambers, one of which had been
occupied by Queen Elizabeth, and another by
James the First, and in both were preserved the
antique beds in which those sovereigns had reposed.

The beds were only used on state occasions,
and their once rich hangings looked dim and
faded, while the rooms themselves, hung with
arras from the looms of Flanders, had a ghostly
air.

All the bed-chambers, as we have intimated,
retained their original furniture. Whether any
of them were haunted we decline to state at
present, but we must own that everybody who
visited the royal apartments declared they must
be haunted, and expressed a decided disinclination
to sleep in them.

There was also a communication from the

gallery, by means of a short staircase, to a private chapel, which was as large as many a country church.

The mansion looked towards the south, and the façade, with its splendid bay windows and richly sculptured portal, was most imposing. A broad terrace, with a stone balustrade, looked down upon the lovely slopes and glades of the park, and ˉcommanded the finest and most extensive prospect imaginable over a lovely district. Some magnificent cedars of Lebanon adorned the lawn.

In the large, old-fashioned gardens, quincunxes, clipped trees, and alleys were to be found; but many modern improvements had been here judiciously introduced.

Not only was Boxgrove a very fine old place, but it was extremely well kept, and this could not have been accomplished without the large establishment that Sir Charles Ilminster maintained.

Sir Charles had already dismounted, and stationed himself at the foot of the broad flight of steps leading to the entrance, when the carriage entered the court.

A bell rung at the gateway brought forth a host of servants, chief among whom was the pompous old butler, Mr. Dancer, who, having served in the house before Sir Charles was born, considered himself the most important person in the establishment, being firmly persuaded that nothing could go on properly without him. Intelligence of the great event of the day, which was likely to produce such an important change in the domestic arrangements of the house, had already reached Boxgrove, being brought by Kennedy, the groom, who had been sent on by his master, and the news, though not wholly unexpected, caused an immense sensation in the household. Some were pleased, but the majority,

we regret to say, were dissatisfied. Among the
latter were the great Mr. Dancer, and Mrs.
Trapp, the housekeeper, neither of whom were
at all desirous of submitting to the dictation of a
young mistress. Mrs. Trapp, who shared with
the butler the rule of the house, did not at all
approve of the choice that Sir Charles had made.
Against the young lady's personal attractions she
had nothing to say—Miss Radcliffe was pretty,
no doubt—but her beauty was insipid, and she
could not for a moment be compared with Lady
Richborough. There was a fascinating woman—
if you please. As to her family, the less said
about them the better. She believed that Miss
Radcliffe had a grandfather, who built Hazlemere,
but she never supposed that the proud Sir Charles
Ilminster, who might have wedded an earl's sister,
would stoop to the daughter of a city merchant.
Pity old Sir Umfraville and her lamented lady-

ship were laid in the family vault. They would
never have allowed the match.

Mr. Dancer attempted to console her by observing that it would certainly have been far
better for Sir Charles—more for his own happiness, and the happiness of all connected with him
—if he would have remained a bachelor; but as
he had allowed himself to be inveigled by an
artful miss-in-her-teens, such an inexperienced girl
might be more easily managed than a woman of
twenty-five. He had always understood that Mrs.
Sutton ruled supreme at Hazlemere, and never
brooked the slightest interference on Miss Radcliffe's part. He recommended Mrs. Trapp to
follow the example set her, which she faithfully
promised to do.

Their colloquy was interrupted by the loud
ringing of the bell at the gate, announcing the

arrival, and summoning Mr. Dancer and a host
of powdered lacqueys to the door.

Chasing away all signs of vexation from her
comely face, Mrs. Trapp prepared to welcome her
future mistress with a smile of delight.

Mrs. Radcliffe and the others had just been
ushered into the hall, when May and those with
her rode into the court. Again Sir Charles was
in attendance on the perron, and assisting his
intended bride to alight, led her into the house.
No one would have supposed, from the profound
respect paid her by the butler, by Mr. Spriggs, the
valet, and the obsequious lacqueys, and the delight
manifested by Mrs. Trapp, who had already made
her appearance in the hall, and was conversing
with Mrs. Radcliffe—no one, we say, could for an
instant have imagined that the slightest objection
had been raised to Sir Charles's choice. Bows and
smiles greeted May on all sides, and certainly her

charming looks and extreme amiability of manner
were calculated to disarm hostility. She addressed
Mrs. Trapp most affably, and that domineering
dame began to think that she should not object
to a young mistress after all. While this was
going on, Colonel Delacombe and Mr. Thornton,
being strangers to the place, were shown round
the ancient hall by Lady Richborough, who
pointed out certain suits of armour, swords, and
bucklers, with histories attached to them, and
called their attention to the portrait of Sir Alberic.
Little time was allowed for this examination. Sir
Charles led the ladies into the dining-room, where
a cold collation was set out, and the rest of the
company followed. The collation was superfluous,
since everybody—except May—had already par-
taken of luncheon; but a glass of wine was
deemed indispensable to the occasion, and Clicquot
and Château Yquem were handed round by Mr.

Dancer and the footmen. Looks full of kindly meaning, and words of kindly import were directed towards May by grandpapa—and not by him alone —as the wine was drunk. Mrs. Sutton was present at the time — very much to the colonel's annoyance, for he felt that her eyes were constantly upon him, and her ears open to everything he said. He owed this infliction to Lady Richborough, who, wishing to show Mrs. Sutton especial attention, insisted upon her remaining with the company. After a second glass of champagne had been quaffed, the survey of the house began.

Mrs. Radcliffe was scarcely equal to the fatiguing task imposed upon her, but she would not be left out, and leaning on Mrs. Sutton's arm, went with the party. Climbing the grand old staircase was indeed a toil, but on reaching the gallery, she sat down, and examined the portraits

with her eye-glass. Mr. Radcliffe, who was standing beside her, could not help remarking in an
undertone what a fine thing it was to be connected with such an ancient and important family
as was here represented. The company were dis-
persed about the gallery. Sir Charles and his
intended had separated themselves from the rest,
and seemed wrapped up in each other's society.
All seemed going on as smoothly and satisfactorily
as those interested in the match could desire, and
papa and grandpapa were enchanted. Unfortunately, Mrs. Radcliffe's delight was marred by a
circumstance which we must proceed to explain.
The inconstant colonel was flirting dreadfully with
Lady Richborough. No mistake about it. There
they were seated together on a velvet-covered
bench at the further end of the gallery — not
looking at the portraits, but looking at each other,
and talking in a very animated manner. If the

colonel was making love, it was clear that he met with plenty of encouragement.

"Upon my word," observed Mr. Radcliffe, greatly amused by what was going on, "I shouldn't be surprised if we have another marriage in the family."

Mrs. Radcliffe had no business to be jealous—but jealous she was—and not being able to contain herself, her angry remarks made her husband laugh very heartily.

"I should have thought, my dear, you would be pleased that the colonel and her ladyship should make a match of it," he said.

"I am disgusted with the flirtation," rejoined his wife. "Do go and put a stop to it."

"Certainly not, my dear," he replied, moving away to examine the pictures.

Another person was likewise jealous—furiously jealous. The day was unpropitious to Oswald.

During the ride to Boxgrove, her ladyship had been entirely engrossed by the colonel, who, sooth to say! seemed enthralled by her fascinations, and had scarcely condescended to notice him. Arrived at the house, she seemed quite unconscious of his presence.

" Decidedly, the colonel has cut you out," remarked Mr. Thornton to his grandson, with affected sympathy.

" Oh! I don't care," cried Oswald. " She is a heartless coquette. She flirted quite as much with me yesterday. To-morrow, it will be the turn of somebody else."

" Sorry for you, notwithstanding," said the old gentleman, with a grave countenance, though he was chuckling internally.

Never for an instant was Mrs. Sutton's gaze removed from the couple whose undisguised flirtation caused such heartburning and jealousy. She watched their looks, and, though at a distance, seemed to divine what passed between them.

Oh! how she hated the fascinating Myrtilla, and if a look would have stricken her dead, she would have so destroyed her. It rejoiced her, however, to feel that Mrs. Radcliffe suffered equally; and the few remarks she made were calculated to inflame her mistress's jealousy. She knew how to plant the sting where it would be felt most keenly.

When at length the colonel and the syren who had charmed him arose, and marching towards Mrs. Radcliffe, inquired "how she liked the pictures?" she had become so agitated that she could scarcely make an intelligible reply. But the colonel did not notice her reproachful look, neither did he appear to trouble himself about Mrs. Sutton.

Very little attention, we are sorry to say, was

paid to the portraits, and the celebrated beauties, proud cavaliers, and gallant gentlemen, ranged along the walls, had never been so shamefully neglected before. The living beauties were the sole objects of attraction—with two, at least, of the party. Sir Charles had eyes only for May —and the infatuated colonel thought Lady Richborough far more charming than Barbara Lady Ilminster, who bloomed in the days of George I., or than the rather décolleté dame who had been admired by James II. when Duke of York, though both were accounted the loveliest women of their time.

Taking Oswald's arm, Mr. Thornton desired him to point out the best portraits. But the wretched young man proved a very indifferent cicerone. He was always either glancing towards May and Sir Charles, or trying to catch some of the colonel's gallant observations to her ladyship.

Generally speaking, much to their credit, the Ilminsters had chosen fair women as their consorts. But there was one notable exception — a great heiress, but not a great beauty. And this lady, the bewildered Oswald informed his grandfather, was the gem of the collection. The old gentleman thought he was joking—but Oswald persisted, till he found out his mistake. It was a relief to the poor fellow when a move was made to the royal bed-chambers, for he then managed to escape from the thraldom in which he had been kept by the old gentleman, but he vainly tried to get a word from Lady Richborough. A visit to the private chapel completed the survey of this part of the mansion, and the party went down stairs.

They then proceeded to the billiard-room, and her ladyship taking down a cue, challenged the colonel, telling him, with a laugh, that she felt

sure she could beat him. Of course, the challenge
was accepted—and, of course, her ladyship was
triumphant—for though a magnificent player, the
colonel did not mean to win. Some betting took
place during the game, and Oswald, who backed
her ladyship, won a couple of sovereigns from his
grand-dad.

The colonel had hoped that he should now be
freed from the jealous surveillance to which he
had been exposed. Vain expectation. Mrs. Radcliffe sat down to watch the game, and, dis-
sembling her rage, extolled Lady Richborough's
play to the skies, declaring she had never seen
anything like it. Mrs. Sutton remained with her
mistress, and her cold grey eyes constantly fixed
upon the colonel rather disturbed his equanimity.
However, he did not desist from paying court to
her ladyship.

Meantime, Sir Charles and his intended had

disappeared. They were in the garden, and remained there so long that Mrs. Radcliffe began to think they were lost, and sent her husband in search of them. He found them slowly returning from a sequestered walk, looking very like a pair of lovers.

Sir Charles was asking a question which he had already asked several times.

"Can you be happy here, dearest May?"

"For the twentieth time, yes," she replied;— "perfectly happy."

Certainly, if vast domains, a magnificent mansion, hosts of servants, and all the accessories of a princely establishment can confer happiness, it might be found at Boxgrove.

But with all its splendour, and all its attractions, May could not have been happy had she not loved Sir Charles. Now nothing dimmed the brightness of the prospect.

Did no thought of Hilary intrude itself? If it did, she banished it on the instant. Why think of him? She had been interested in him —nothing more. A momentary dream. He must be forgotten. Union with him was out of the question.

Sir Charles felt he should be the happiest of men possessed of one so bright and pure—so utterly untainted by the world—as the fair nymph he had chosen. He loved her passionately — with a love that a proud and loyal heart like his alone can feel—and he vowed to devote his life to her.

Not liking to part with his visitors, Sir Charles proposed that they should stay dinner. Mrs. Radcliffe objected, declaring she could not venture to remain out so late. Besides, dinner had been ordered at home. Why not go back with them, and dine at Hazlemere?

Agreed to at once. Provided he was not separated from the object of his idolatry, Sir Charles did not care what arrangement was made. But he could not give up the supreme delight of riding back with May. Accordingly, evening dresses for himself and his sister were ordered to be sent on in the brougham, under the care of Mr. Spriggs. Pleading fatigue, Mrs. Radcliffe begged that her carriage might come round in an hour, and directions were given to that effect.

Colonel Delacombe must see the stables—the hunters were worth seeing, as he would find. So, Sir Charles being too much occupied to go with him, her ladyship volunteered to show them to him herself, and Mr. Thornton played the part of propriety and went with them.

Luckily, they were free from Mrs. Radcliffe, who would as soon have entered a dungeon as a stable. However, in this instance she need

not have been so mighty particular, for the
stables of Boxgrove, which were personally su-
perintended by Lady Richborough, were admirably kept—cleaner, her ladyship declared, than
any drawing-room. A pair of bull-terriers belong-
ing to Thorpe, the coachman, came out to greet
her, and attended her during the inspection. She
did the honours of the stable, if we may so speak,
with inimitable grace; begged the gentlemen to
do as they pleased in regard to a cigar. She
didn't object to one. Sir Charles always smoked
when he went over the stables with her. So they
gladly availed themselves of the permission.

Attended by a couple of active young grooms,
who obeyed her slightest gesture, she then led
them from stall to stall. How well the horses
knew her. What whinnying, what rattling of
halters at the sound of her voice. A pretty sight
to see her standing beside a favourite courser

patting his satin coat, and proclaiming his merits. Pleasant to listen to her, while she dilated with flashing eyes upon the performances of the noble animal, who seemed to comprehend what she said, and testified his satisfaction as she told of his wondrous feats.

Sir Charles had a first-rate stud—not an indifferent horse in the collection. The colonel was in raptures, and would have been well content to remain for some time longer in the stables, especially in such delightful society.

But before the examination could be completed, they were summoned away. The landau had gone round, and the horses were being saddled. Go they must. Mrs. Radcliffe could not be kept waiting. Indeed, her ladyship felt she had neglected her shockingly.

That Mrs. Radcliffe was impatient to be off was manifest. Already she was in the carriage with Mrs. Sutton by her side, and her husband opposite her. The old gentleman's seat was the only one vacant. Into it he got as quickly as he could, for he discerned a frown on his daughter's brow. Lady Richborough was profuse in her apologies, but Mrs. Radcliffe smiled blandly and begged her not to say a word about it. It was very proper the colonel should see the stables, and she herself had been greatly amused by looking about the rooms; in fact, she had spent a most delightful day. She waved her hand to Sir Charles and May, who were standing on the steps, and the carriage drove off.

Scarcely had it passed through the great gateway than the horses were brought round. Lady Richborough, though she wanted no assistance, allowed the colonel to assist her to the saddle. Kissing the silver handle of her whip to May, and glancing archly at her brother, she then

rode off, escorted as before by the colonel and
Oswald.   Our young friend, who it must be
owned, had been infamously treated, was now in
the sulks, and as soon as they gained the park
he dropped behind under pretence of lighting a
cigar, and then, without making an effort to
overtake them, dashed off in a different direction.
Poor fellow! we are concerned to say that his
absence was not regretted.

"How very obliging of that dear Oswald to re-
lieve us of his company," observed the colonel,
laughing.

"I fear I must have slightly hurt his feelings,"
said her ladyship, displaying her pearls.

"Never mind! he won't break his heart —
though mine would be broken if I were so
treated."

"I very much doubt if you have a heart to
break," cried her ladyship.   "Allons! I will take

you back through a different part of the park.
We will go through the woods."

" Through the woods—charming!" cried the
colonel.

Their course led them through some of the
most secluded portions of the park, and after
passing through the walnut and chesnut groves,
previously mentioned, they were involved in a
thicket which covered the lower part of the hill.
The road, edged on either side by tall pines, was
so narrow that they were obliged to proceed singly.
However, this did not prevent the colonel, who
brought up the rear, from addressing many a
gallant speech to his fair companion. These could
not have been very disagreeable to her, for ever
and anon she turned a smiling face towards him,
and at such moments looked irresistibly charming.

They were still in the midst of the thicket, when
a tall young man was seen ascending the narrow

road clothed in a grey Tweed suit, and having a knapsack at his back. He seemed to require the aid of the stout stick which he grasped.

On seeing her ladyship he halted for a moment, and then came on. Owing to the interposition of the foremost horse, he could not distinguish the colonel, neither did the colonel perceive him. Her ladyship, however, shook her whip at her companion to check the rapturous speech he had just commenced, and he took the hint without exactly knowing why silence was enjoined.

As Lady Richborough drew near, the young man stepped out of the road to allow her passage. Leaning against a lofty pine for support, he raised his felt hat to salute her, revealing pallid but singularly handsome features, that startled her as she gazed on them.

In an instant she recovered from her surprise, and courteously returning the salutation, passed on. Looking back, she perceived, from the

colonel's manner, that the stranger was not unknown to him. What surprised her still more
was, that the colonel's countenance had assumed a
very stern expression. He was evidently put out
by the unexpected rencounter.

Reining in her steed, she said,

"You appear to know that young man, colonel.
May I ask who he is?"

"I know very little about him," he replied,
carelessly. "I met him this morning at Hazlemere. An artist, I believe, by name Hilary St.
Ives."

"That Hilary St. Ives?" cried her ladyship.
"Now, indeed, I am surprised. Do call him back.
I should like so much to speak to him."

"Your ladyship must excuse me if I decline
to obey your behest," rejoined the colonel. "I
can have nothing to do with that young fellow."

"Oh, indeed!" exclaimed her ladyship.

She saw something was wrong. But the

colonel's manner did not encourage her to ask any further questions, and though still full of curiosity, she desisted.

But how came Hilary in Boxgrove Park? Above all, how came he in that secluded road, known to few, and frequented by none save inmates of the mansion?

The thought perplexed her strangely.

VIII.

HILARY'S LETTER.

A DISAGREEABLE surprise, as we are aware, awaited Mrs. Radcliffe on her return to Hazle-mere.

As she entered her boudoir, she learnt from Annette, who was in attendance, that Hilary had taken his departure.

" The young gentleman left quite sudden, mem, about an hour and a half after you had started for Boxgrove, without mentioning his intention

to any one—except me. He went away on foot,
with a knapsack on his back."

"But surely he left some message for me?"

"Only this letter, mem, which he desired me
to lay on your table. No doubt it will give you
all perticklers."

Mrs. Radcliffe looked at the letter, but, much
to Annette's disappointment, did not open it,
deferring its perusal till she should be quite
alone.

"I haven't time to read it now," she said. "I
must dress for dinner at once. Lady Richborough will require your services presently. Her
ladyship dines here to-day, and will dress on her
arrival."

"Yes, mem, I knows. Mr. Spriggs have
brought her la'yship's evening dress in the broom,
and I've put it out all ready for her in Miss
May's dressing-room. A sweet pretty dress it is,

mem, as ever I see, and I'm sure her la'yship
will look charming in it, as she do in everything
she wears."

Annette was not all prepared for the pique
exhibited by her mistress at this observation.
She followed her into the dressing-room, which
communicated by a side-door with the boudoir.
The dressing-room was very tastefully fitted up,
with a large cheval glass hung with muslin, and
a toilette-table covered with old lace, on which
reposed numberless flacons of perfumes, boxes of
pearl-powder and iris-powder, and pots of fard.

"Look out my prettiest dress, Annette," said
Mrs. Radcliffe, seating herself in a chaise longue.
"I must not be entirely eclipsed by her lady-
ship."

"No fear of that, mem," replied Annette, eager
to repair the error she had committed. "I always
says, and Mrs. Sutton will bear me out, that

for grace and style—let alone good looks—no one can come up to our own dear lady."

"You are a silly creature, Annette, and I ought not to listen to such ridiculous flattery," said Mrs. Radcliffe, smiling. "My day is gone by."

"Oh no, mem, I can't allow that. Any one would take you for Miss May's elder sister."

"Bah! Choose the dress that you think will become me most. I really want to look well to-night."

"Then wear your white satin robe with the yellow satin panier, mem. You will put a complete distinguisher on her la'yship's pink dress."

Precisely what Mrs. Radcliffe desired. So the dress recommended was adopted, and very charming her mistress looked in it, Annette declared.

Her task ended, Annette was departing, when Mrs. Radcliffe stopped her to inquire whether Mr. St. Ives had given any directions respecting his chest.

"No, mem, he said nothing about it, and I didn't think to ask him; but after he was gone I went to his room, and the first thing I see was the chest. The key was in it, so I thought there could be no harm in taking a peep at its contents. It was nearly full of linen and clothes —fine shirts as ever you see, mem, and spick-and-span new coats and waistcoats. I don't know what else there might be, for I had seen quite enough, and locking up the chest I put the key in my pocket, intending to give it to Mrs. Sutton on her return."

"Quite right. But don't give it her just now. She is busy about dinner, and this unexpected occurrence will put her out very much—as it does me."

"Begging your pardon, mem, Mrs. Sutton must have heard of the young gentleman's sudden departure from Mr. Luff. All the servants have been talking about it."

"Well, go and see after her ladyship. She must have arrived by this time. Make her look as charming as you can."

"You have nothing to fear from her, mem, I can assure you," rejoined Annette, as she quitted the room.

Mrs. Radcliffe then passed into the boudoir.

After a moment's hesitation, she opened Hilary's letter. The bank-notes dropped out upon the table and alarmed her, and her agitation increased as she read as follows:

"MADAM,—You desired me to await your return, but I cannot do so, for reasons which I shall proceed to state.

"I hope I shall not pain you by what I have to say. I would not wound the feelings of one to whom I owe so much, and for whom I feel such strong affection. But I must speak plainly, lest my conduct should be misunderstood.

" The mystery of my birth is no longer a mystery. Brought hither by fate, when proceeding in a different direction in quest of information, I have unexpectedly learnt the secret. But the knowledge thus strangely acquired has been dearly purchased. My true position has been revealed to me. I now know *why* I am disowned, and *why* I can never be acknowledged.

" Judging by my own emotions, I can guess what yours must have been, when carried away by excitement, you allowed the secret, which you have so long and so carefully kept, to escape your lips. The avowal, I know, was made unconsciously, and perhaps would have been recalled, had recal been possible. Would it had never been made !

" What extravagances I might have committed in the delirium of the moment, but for the interruption caused by your husband's entrance, I cannot tell. No wonder I was scarcely master of myself, when I obtained the certitude that the mother whom I supposed to be dead was living and standing before me.

"But when my transports subsided, reflection convinced me that I had better have remained in ignorance of the secret.

"The discovery could profit me nothing. The necessity for concealment was strong as ever— stronger perhaps. No disclosure of my parentage could possibly be made without damage to the honour and happiness of others. I must remain what I am. On no consideration would I bring disgrace upon you, or upon those with whom you are connected.

"Were I to stay here longer I should not only offend your husband, for whom I entertain great respect, and from whom I have experienced great kindness, but I might also unintentionally imperil you. Prudence, therefore, enjoins my immediate departure. Another interview with you might shake the good resolutions I have formed.

"Some things connected with my history still perplex me, and these you might have explained. But I shall institute no further inquiries. I have learnt enough—too much, alas!

"You may desire to know what I propose to do. I shall strive to achieve an independence. I have marked out a career for myself which I shall steadily and unflinchingly pursue. Relying for success entirely upon my own energies, I can accept no further aid, even from those who may deem it a duty to aid me.

"Acting upon this resolve, I must respectfully decline Colonel Delacombe's late presents in money and clothing, and beg to return them to him, through you. Though poor enough, Heaven knows! I do not require the large sum he has

thought proper to send me—nor any portion of
it. My own hand will maintain me.

"One thing more. As I shall never bear his
arms, even with a bend sinister, his signet-ring
will be useless to me. Pray restore it to him.
I do not now need the evidence it affords of my
birth.

"In acting thus, do not suppose I am influenced
by pride, or galled by the sense of injustice. I
have no right to be proud; and if I have suffered
wrong I can endure it without a murmur. I am
actuated by feelings which, if I could explain
them, would, I am sure, command your respect.

"To say that I can ever become reconciled to
my enforced position would be idle and untrue.
But I must learn to submit.

"Henceforth, I stand alone.

"Farewell, madam! Think of me sometimes,
I pray you. I shall always think of you—always

with affection. We may never meet again —
better we should not—but rest assured whatever
betide, you will never have reason to blush for
him who is, unfortunately, compelled to subscribe
himself,

"HILARY ST. IVES."

The perusal of this letter roused extraordinary
emotions in Mrs. Radcliffe's breast, and she was
still under their dominion when Mrs. Sutton
entered the boudoir. The housekeeper's haggard
looks alarmed her mistress.

"Don't agitate me, Sutton, I beseech you.
My nerves have been dreadfully shattered by this
letter. Read it before you say a word."

The housekeeper sat down, and it was well she
did so, for she had not read many lines when her
strength completely failed her. A mist gathered
before her eyes, but she brushed aside her tears

and went on. Internal agony was plainly de-
picted in her countenance, and excited Mrs. Radcliffe's commiseration. But the housekeeper re-
sented her sympathy.

"This is all your fault!" she cried. "The
error you have committed may appear trifling,
but it is fraught with fearful consequences, which
cannot be repaired. You have led him to believe
you are his mother, and he has gone away with
that conviction. How is he to be disabused?
You cannot find him. You cannot communicate
with him. See what you have done. By an
inconsiderate word you have deprived him of the
few friends he possesses, and have thrown him
upon the world without resources. For whatever
misfortunes may happen to him you will be
responsible. He tells you that you have made
him wretched, and the whole tenor of his letter
proves that he is so."

"Peace, Sutton, peace! I cannot endure this. No misfortunes shall happen to him. I can still find means of aiding him."

"But he will not accept your assistance."

"He can be aided indirectly. The colonel will devise some plan for his benefit."

"The colonel will do nothing for him. I am sure of it."

"You are unjust towards the colonel, Sutton. He has shown every disposition to help the poor young man."

"How?" demanded the housekeeper, sceptically.

"Has he not just sent him five hundred pounds and an expensive outfit? What further proof do you need of the interest he takes in Hilary's welfare?"

Mrs. Sutton could make no rejoinder.

"No one could have foreseen the unfortunate

turn that things have taken," pursued Mrs. Radcliffe. "Hilary's pride—though, like all proud
people, he denies that he has any pride—is a
stumbling-block in the way of his advancement.
I fear also that he is wanting in gratitude. I
observe with pain that he does not allude to you
in his letter. I trust he has written to bid you
farewell, and thank you for your great kindness
to him."

"He has not written to me," rejoined the
housekeeper, with difficulty repressing a pang.

"He is much to blame for the neglect. But his
thoughts, no doubt, were occupied with me, whom
he looks upon as his mother. A strange mistake,
and yet not surprising—all things considered."

"It is not surprising at all, after what you
have said to him," cried the housekeeper, sharply.
"He is gone. Let him take his own course."

"No, I cannot desert him. I must watch over

him—unseen, unknown. You shall act for me, Sutton."

"I can make no promise."

"You are hurt by his ingratitude towards you, and I don't wonder at it. But you must make allowances for him. We will talk more on the subject to-morrow. Meantime, I must put these things by."

"I should like to read that letter again. Leave it with me, if you are going down-stairs."

"Excuse me, dear Sutton. I know the letter would be safe with you. But I cannot trust it out of my own custody."

As she spoke, she locked up the letter and the roll of bank-notes in a tiroir of the bureau.

If she could have seen the look bestowed upon her by the housekeeper while she was thus employed, she would not have gone down to dinner with as much composure as she did.

IX.

A LITTLE MUSIC IN THE DRAWING-ROOM, AND A LITTLE TALK IN THE DRESSING-ROOM.

No one would have suspected from Mrs. Radcliffe's looks and manner during dinner that anything was on her mind. Greatly disturbed by Hilary's abrupt departure, her jealousy was again excited by the colonel's continued attentions to Lady Richborough. Yet her countenance had a placid expression, and a smile was upon her lips. Despite all Annette's efforts, she was completely thrown into the shade by her ladyship, who looked surprisingly well in an evening dress. White as Parian marble, Myrtilla's lovely neck and shoulders might have served as a model for a sculptor, while the classical mould of her features would have suggested a representation of the goddesss of the silver bow. She was in high spirits, and though her sweetest smiles and most bewitching glances were bestowed upon the colonel, she dispensed her fascinations around, and did not even neglect poor Oswald. In short, she was extremely useful as well as highly ornamental, and communicated a vast deal of life and spirit to the party, which might have flagged without her aid, for Sir Charles talked only to May.

Her ladyship's curiosity having been excited by the rencounter in the morning, she brought up the subject of Hilary St. Ives. But no one seemed inclined to talk about him. Mr. Radcliffe

could give no explanation of his sudden departure; and Mr. Thornton shrugged his shoulders when questioned. He knew nothing about
the young fellow, and was heartily glad he was
gone. That was all he had to say. Very strange.
She thought Mrs. Radcliffe could tell her something, and resolved to seek an explanation from
her in private.

Dinner excellent. The cabinet Johannisberg
warmed grandpapa's heart, and the '20 port,
which appeared with the dessert, put him into a
blissful state. Apropos of the dessert! we may
be permitted to mention that Macdonald's straw-
berries were magnificent, and Sir Charles told
Mrs. Radcliffe that he must certainly carry away
her gardener.

The health of the queen of the fête was of
course drunk in bumpers, and the few words
uttered on the occasion by grandpapa caused a

good deal of laughter, and raised some blushes on May's cheek.

Soon afterwards the ladies retired, and the gentlemen quickly followed them — much too quickly for Mr. Thornton, who had not half finished his bottle of '20 port. He hated to be hurried in this way. Why should not a man be allowed to enjoy his wine?—especially wine like this.

" Do tell me something about this mysterious Hilary St. Ives?" said Lady Richborough to Mrs. Radcliffe, as they entered the drawing-room together.

" He is an artist, that is all I know about him," was the evasive reply.

" But why has he left you so suddenly?"

" Grandpapa and the colonel objected to him. I know no other reason."

" Oh! the colonel objected to him!—that's

odd ! Do you know that I was very much struck
by his likeness to the colonel."

"Have you seen him, then ?"

"Yes. As the colonel and I were riding back
through one of the thickets in the park, we came
upon him quite unexpectedly. I had not the
slightest idea who he was at the moment—but
the likeness startled me."

"Strange you should meet him there? What
could he be doing in the park ?"

"Just what I want to know. Does he intend
to remain in the neighbourhood ?"

"I should think not. I fancy he is going to
town to practise his profession."

"Boxgrove is out of the way, if he was going
to town. He must have had some motive to take
him there."

"I can conceive none, unless he desired to take
some views of the park. It is certainly strange

he should be there. If you see him again, or hear anything more of him, pray inform me."

"Aha! she takes an interest in him, I perceive," thought her ladyship. "There must be some reason for his sudden departure."

Naturally, she promised compliance, and then added quickly, "You will think I am troubling you with questions—but tell me! Is Colonel Delacombe a widower? You are aware I have seen him for the first time to-day, and know very little of him except by report as a distinguished officer."

Guessing the object of the inquiry, Mrs. Radcliffe could not help smiling.

"A widower! no!" she rejoined. "Colonel Delacombe has never been married. I can state that positively."

Her ladyship appeared very well satisfied by the assurance.

"What are you talking about?" asked May, joining them.

Before replying, Lady Richborough consulted Mrs. Radcliffe by a glance, that seemed to say, "Shall I tell her?" and received a look signifying, "Better not."

She therefore answered, "I have been propounding a riddle, which mamma finds it difficult to solve. Come to the piano. I want to practise a duet with you before the gentlemen appear."

The evening passed off delightfully. Lady Richborough was so much occupied at the piano, that she could not flirt with the colonel, though she held him in thrall by her voice, and ever and anon electrified him with a glance. Consequently, Mrs. Radcliffe was quite easy, and able to enjoy the music. Oswald likewise, who had been unmercifully rallied by his grandsire, put on a cheerful air, and accompanied the ladies on the cornet-à-piston.

Myrtilla in a riding-habit, on horseback, or in the stable—laughing, jesting, indulging in a little harmless slang, and tolerant of a cigar; Myrtilla in the drawing-room, in a costume not calculated to conceal her splendid neck and shoulders—dazzling, refined, accomplished—so different was her ladyship under the two aspects, that she scarcely resembled the same person.

If the colonel was captivated by the fair equestrian, whose predilection for the stable and fondness for its occupants in no way displeased him, he was perfectly fascinated by the grace and accomplishments of the high-bred dame. Conscious that she looked well at the piano, Myrtilla enthroned herself before the instrument during the evening. Gifted with a rich contralto voice, she sang the "brindisi" almost as well as Alboni, and completed her performance by a grand fantasia, which she executed with wonderful brilliancy.

The colonel and Mr. Thornton were transported, and expressed their delight with enthusiasm, but Sir Charles, who was accustomed to his sister's wondrous performances, very much preferred a simple ballad, which was exquisitely sung by May. It held him breathless as he listened.

Delightful as it was, the evening came to an end. Before the party separated, arrangements were made for next day. Everybody was to dine at Boxgrove, and come over early if the day should prove fine—to play at croquet, or ramble about the park.

Mrs. Radcliffe, as usual, feared it would be too much for her, but promised to come, nevertheless. What laughing there was in the hall! And how Sir Charles envied his sister the kiss she received from May as she bade her good night!

The colonel had a tender word for her ladyship, and gently squeezed her hand, while leading her to the brougham.

"Well, dear boy!" cried Myrtilla, as they were borne swiftly towards Boxgrove, "I can really and truly congratulate you. You will have the sweetest wife in England. But what's to become of poor me, when you are married?"

"Why you will live with us, of course," he rejoined.

"Not at all of course. Perhaps, your wife won't like me."

"Nonsense! you know better."

Her ladyship appeared abstracted for a moment, and then tapping him with her fan, said, "Light a cigar. Don't go to sleep."

"I never was less inclined to sleep," he rejoined.

"What do you think of Colonel Delacombe?" she asked, rather abruptly.

" What do *you* think of him, Myrtilla ? That's more to the purpose," he rejoined, with a laugh. " Are you disposed to return with him to India ?"

" I shouldn't altogether dislike it. I suppose he is well off. Find out all about him for me, dear boy."

Sir Charles told her there was no necessity to make any inquiries respecting an officer so well known and so distinguished as Colonel Delacombe. Thereupon, he lighted a manilla, and her ladyship fell into a reverie, which lasted till they reached the house.

Here we shall leave them, and return to May, who had already retired to her dressing-room, and while preparing for rest was ruminating upon the events of the day, when a gentle tap at the door announced the housekeeper.

" Oh, Sutton, I'm so glad to see you !" cried May. " I want to know what has happened to poor Hilary St. Ives. Annette tells me he has left a letter for mamma. You have seen it, of course?"

"Yes, but there are secrets in it, which I am not permitted to disclose."

"Secrets! Dear me, how dreadfully mysterious! You quite rouse my curiosity. Am I not to know a little bit of the letter?" she said, in a coaxing tone.

"No, I daren't speak. Besides, you can't take any interest in the poor young man now."

"You are mistaken, Sutton, I take the greatest interest in him—in his welfare, I mean. I have been thinking of something for him."

"Indeed!"

"Yes. Our portraits—that is, the portraits of Sir Charles and myself—are to be placed in the great gallery, which you visited this morning, Sutton. I mean Hilary to paint them."

"But will Sir Charles consent?"

"Sir Charles will do anything I like. He will be delighted to encourage genius."

"I fear he will not have an opportunity of doing so in Hilary's case. The poor young man is gone. He does not desire to be heard of more. I suspect he means to change his name."

"Well, I must say it is very stupid of him— very annoying—just when I had arranged it all so nicely."

"He could know nothing of your kind intentions. But I don't think he would have painted the portraits."

"Yes, I'm sure he would—if I had asked him," she cried, in a tone of pique. "I'm quite angry with him for being so foolish."

"Do you recollect our conversation before breakfast this morning, dear?" said Mrs. Sutton, fixing an inquiring look upon her. "Are you quite satisfied with what you have done since? Don't be afraid of confiding in me."

"Yes, dear Sutton, my feelings are entirely changed since morning. I have discovered that I can love Sir Charles—nay, I *do* love him. All his noble qualities have been revealed to me, and I am surprised I should have been so long blind to them."

" When did you make the discovery?—at Boxgrove?" inquired the housekeeper, in an ironical tone.

"You think me inconstant, I perceive, but I am not so. This morning my heart was perfectly disengaged—and I own I should not have listened to Sir Charles except on his sister's persuasion. I now know him better than I did. As I first looked into his eyes, I read truth and loyalty in them—and such devotion, Sutton. I am sure he would lay down his life for me if I required it. He said so."

" A mere phrase !" cried the housekeeper, with an ill-disguised sneer. " All men say so."

" It was not an idle phrase with him, but of course I don't mean to put his devotion to the proof."

" No, that wouldn't be prudent. You would lose Boxgrove."

" It strikes me, Sutton, that you are not pleased that I have accepted Sir Charles."

" All I desire is your happiness, dear."

" Then rest easy. I shall be perfectly happy with him."

" At all events, you will be Lady Ilminster— mistress of one of the most splendid seats in the county, and while elevating yourself, you will have the satisfaction of feeling that you have elevated your own family."

" I don't exactly like what you say, Sutton, nor the tone in which you say it. I know that

I love Sir Charles—not for his title—not for Boxgrove—but for *himself*—though you would imply the contrary—and I am sure I shall be happy with him."

"Well, I hope so. Good night, dear! May your slumbers be light and pleasant."

As she left the room she muttered to herself, "Impossible to shake her! She is as worldly as her mother."

"Something is the matter with Sutton to-night," thought May, as she was left alone. "She appears to be put out by poor Hilary's departure. Well, I am sorry I cannot help him, but perhaps it is better he is gone."

Shortly afterwards she sought her couch, and sweet dreams springing from a pure and gentle heart hovered above her pillow.

Thus ended May's nineteenth birthday.

X.

THE COLONEL'S OPINION OF THE LETTER.

NEXT morning Mrs. Radcliffe did not make her appearance at breakfast. Nor could this be wondered at, after the fatigue she had undergone on the previous day. Besides, she had another fatiguing day in prospect.

However, she sent a message by Mrs. Sutton to Colonel Delacombe, begging him to come up to her boudoir after breakfast, as she wished to have a little conversation with him.

To hear was to obey. Though for many

reasons the colonel would willingly have avoided the proposed tête-à-tête.

On repairing to the boudoir, he found the lady reclining in her accustomed fauteuil near the fire —for there was still a fire, though the day was bright and warm—got up for the occasion in an elegant dishabille. Languor in her manner, reproach in her looks.

Saluting him in a faint—very faint—voice, she did not attempt to rise—that would have been too great an effort—or even offer him her hand, though he hesitated not to take it. She prayed him to be seated, but the colonel preferred standing with his back to the fire, regarding her with what he intended for a strong expression of sympathy.

Neither of them dreamed that the door communicating with the dressing-room, which was concealed by a screen, was left slightly ajar, and that the person stationed behind it could hear, and *did* hear, all that passed.

"I am afraid you rather overdid it yesterday, Esther," said the colonel. "You look sadly jaded."

"Yes; but I am suffering from low spirits— not fatigue."

"Low spirits! This is not the time to indulge in the vapours when you have made such a capital hit with your daughter. You have got everything you could desire. Boxgrove is really the finest old place I ever saw, and Sir Charles is excessively gentlemanlike and agreeable."

"Yes, I don't complain. I am perfectly satisfied with May's choice. Apropos of Sir Charles! what do you think of his sister?" demanded the lady, fixing her eye-glass upon him.

"Now it's coming," he thought. "A very fine woman. Time was when I should have fallen desperately in love with her."

"Time *was*, Seymour!" cried the lady, re-proachfully. "Say, rather, time *is*. It appears to me that you are just as impressionable as ever. I was grieved to see you make such a ridiculous exhibition of yourself yesterday. You fancy her ladyship is struck. My poor, dear, deluded friend, she was only trifling with you, as you will find to your cost, if you think at all seriously of a heartless coquette, who flirts with every man she meets. You saw how she treated Oswald. Well, the day before she was flirting violently with him, and half turned the poor boy's head. I suppose you know she loses her jointure if she marries again?"

"A hint to that effect was given me by Mr. Thornton. But what is her jointure to me? I don't care about it."

"But you care a great deal about the lovely widow—that is evident. Nay, no protestations to the contrary. They won't pass with me. Listen,"

she exclaimed, altering her manner. "You shall
not say that I am in the way. I release you
from your vow. But for your own sake, Seymour, as you value your peace and comfort, don't
choose Myrtilla. She will drive you frantic with
jealousy."

The colonel laughed carelessly.

"A capital joke," he cried. "I rather fancy
I can take care of myself. Her ladyship may
use a needle-gun, but since I shall keep out of
range, she won't hurt me."

And he again laughed gaily.

Mrs. Radcliffe shook her head and sighed:

"Ah, you men — you men! base deceivers
ever! But to change the theme. I have a letter
to show you."

"A letter!" he exclaimed, with internal misgiving. "I hate letters. For one that is pleasant
we get a dozen disagreeable."

"I am sorry to inflict this upon you, but you must see it. It is from Hilary St. Ives."

"From him! ha!" cried the colonel, knitting his brows.

Seating himself, he read the letter deliberately, without making a remark, but his looks grew sterner as he went on.

" This would be laughable were it not serious !" he cried, tossing down the letter angrily when he had done. "I suppose we must treat it seriously, though it scarcely deserves to be so treated. The young fellow seems half crazed. The knock on the pate that he got from the gipsies must have confused his intellects. Several points require ex-planation."

"You can best explain one point, Seymour," rejoined Mrs. Radcliffe. "Pardon me if I put a direct question to you. The circumstances of the case must plead my excuse. You may be perfectly frank with me. Have you any reason to believe this young man to be your son?"

"Pardon me, my dear Esther, if I reply by another question. Have *you* any reason to believe yourself to be his mother?"

"For shame, Seymour!" she cried, with affected indignation. "This is too bad."

"Not a bit worse than the accusation you bring against me."

"Well, I have another interrogation to put. Since you deny the parentage, pray, what was your motive for sending him the five hundred pounds and the outfit?"

"On my honour, I have sent him neither."

"But here are the bank notes to confute you, and the clothes-chest is in his room."

"Another hand has been at work—not mine," he rejoined, gravely. "This is a most vexatious business, and you yourself — from the best of motives—have contrived to complicate it. With regard to the money which you suppose came from me, I advise you to commit it to the keeping of Mrs. Sutton. She may find an opportunity of communicating with the young man. But do not meddle further in the matter yourself. You have already done too much."

"I will act as you suggest. I don't like the charge of the money. One more question and I have done. How came your signet-ring in Hilary's possession?"

"Now, I confess you puzzle me. I can only answer that I lost the ring many years ago— before I went out to India."

"Before you knew me, Seymour?'"

"Why that question? Yes. It may have been stolen from me with some such design as has just been put in practice. Are you satisfied?"

"I must be. May I keep the ring?"

" Certainly. But let me burn that letter. It compromises you most seriously."

The person outside the door was upon the point of rushing into the room to prevent, at all hazards, the destruction of the letter, but Mrs. Radcliffe's answer checked her.

" No, I can't allow you to burn it," she cried, snatching the letter from him. " No one shall see it."

" This is downright madness," cried the colonel. " Suppose the letter were to fall into your husband's hands, what would he think of it ?"

" Such an event will never occur. Mr. Radcliffe never opens any of my drawers."

The colonel did not look half satisfied, but he saw it was useless to remonstrate further, for Mrs. Radcliffe proceeded to lock up the letter, the bank-notes, and the ring.

" There, they are all safe now !" she cried.

"I hope Mrs. Sutton has not got a key of that drawer," he remarked.

"No, no. This is the only key I don't trust her with."

"You trust her a great deal too much, Esther. Be cautious."

"My dear Seymour, she is fidelity itself, and would never betray a secret of mine."

"Then her looks belie her. I am a physiognomist, you know, and I warn you against her. She is treacherous."

"Treacherous! why, you have just advised me to give her the five hundred pounds."

"Because I would rather she had it than you. Hist!" he cried, "I thought I heard a noise."

As the words were uttered the dressing-room door was softly closed.

Just in time, for the colonel looked over the top of the screen, but of course made no discovery.

"Where is Mrs. Sutton?" he asked.

"I don't know. Possibly in my dressing-room. She went there just before you came in. Have you anything to say to her?"

"Merely a word."

"Just touch the bell then."

The colonel did as enjoined, and shortly afterwards Mrs. Sutton made her appearance.

The colonel fixed a stern and searching look upon her.

"Your mistress has some money to give you," he said. "You will know what to do with it."

The housekeeper looked inquiringly at Mrs. Radcliffe.

"Yes, the money sent to Hilary. You understand, Sutton. The colonel thinks you ought to have charge of it."

"Yes, and the clothes-chest too. Take care of that. And see that your mistress is no further troubled."

"Is Colonel Delacombe master here?" said the housekeeper to Mrs. Radcliffe. "Am I to take his orders or yours?"

"You will be pleased to take mine now," said the colonel, with a look that crushed her, as he quitted the room.

XI.

A SKETCH TAKEN IN BOXGROVE PARK.

By the time the colonel got down-stairs he
had quite recovered his composure, and was able
to offer a very cheerful greeting to Sir Charles,
who had arrived during his absence. This early
visit was not included in the arrangements of the
day, but was none the less agreeable because
unexpected. The only thing that marred the
colonel's satisfaction was that her ladyship had
been left behind. Far too considerate to interrupt a tête-à-tête, already commenced by the

lovers in the drawing-room, he strolled out into the garden to smoke a cigar, and think matters over.

His meditations were chiefly occupied by Myrtilla, of whom, notwithstanding his assertions to Mrs. Radcliffe, he had become violently enamoured; and though he entertained no doubt that her captivating ladyship was the coquette she had been represented, he did not feel uneasy on that account. Vanity whispered that she wouldn't throw him over. She was just the person to suit him. Such a wife would give him additional éclat. Her unrivalled beauty would create an immense sensation in India. He didn't care how much she was admired. Esther declared he would be frightfully jealous. Bah! He laughed at the idea. His was not a jealous nature. But hold! he was getting on rather too fast. There was a trifling difficulty in the way that had to be removed—a difficulty that he could not have foreseen a few days ago. The consideration of this difficulty, which to any other than the colonel would have appeared insurmountable, necessitated a second cigar—even a third. Nor when that was consumed had he arrived at a satisfactory conclusion.

At last, he resolved to ride over by himself to Boxgrove, and have a talk with her ladyship. Having communicated his design to Mr. Radcliffe, that gentleman ordered a horse to be brought round for him at once.

However, we will mount a courser fleeter than any in our respected friend's stables, and speeding to Boxgrove, ascertain what the lovely Myrtilla was about.

It may be asked why she did not accompany her brother? To this we must reply that Sir Charles did not particularly desire her company.

A real lover, when not in the society of the mistress of his heart, wishes to be alone.

Her ladyship rode with him to the lodge-gates, and then receiving a hint to the above effect, quitted him, and continued to take exercise within the park, riding about in different directions for some time.

Her thoughts, we may be permitted to say, were occupied with the colonel, and she was considering whether it would be worth while to accept him.

All at once, she caught sight of a figure among a grove of trees which at once fixed her attention.

The person she beheld was seated upon the root of a large beech-tree, and was evidently sketching the mansion, which could be very well seen from the position he had selected.

Entertaining no doubt that the sketcher was Hilary St. Ives, she determined to have a word

with him. Bashfulness, as we are aware, was not
her ladyship's foible. A circuitous route brought
her to the back of the wood, and she came upon
him by surprise. He was so much engrossed by
his task that he did not notice her approach till
she was close beside him. When he perceived
her, he arose in some confusion, and took off
his hat to salute her.

"Do not let me interrupt you, I beg," she
said, with a gracious smile. And wishing to put
him completely at his ease, she added, "Mr.
Hilary St. Ives, I believe.'

Bowing assent, he rejoined, "I am afraid I
am an intruder; but I was so struck with this
fine old mansion yesterday that I could not quit
the neighbourhood without making a sketch of it."

"Will you allow me to look at the sketch?"

"With the greatest pleasure. But I fear it
won't please you. I haven't satisfied myself."

"I like it very much," she rejoined. "I don't see how it could be improved. Many sketches have been taken of the old place, but I like none so much as this. I think you have chosen the best view of the place."

"Every view of the mansion is picturesque and striking. It would make a dozen capital pictures."

"Can I prevail upon you to execute them? I will endeavour to make it worth your while to oblige me."

"I should be delighted to do your bidding, and without other reward than such commendation as you have bestowed upon this worthless sketch. But I am going away immediately."

"The delay of a day or two cannot much matter, I should think," she remarked, with a captivating smile.

"Your ladyship may be quite sure that if I

had not good reason for declining, I would not hesitate to obey you."

"You know me, I perceive."

"Once seen, your ladyship is not likely to be forgotten. I caught a glimpse of you at Hazlemere yesterday, and later on I was fortunate enough to meet you in one of the thickets of this park."

"Yes. Colonel Delacombe told me your name. I had heard of you previously."

She looked at him as she made the observation, and perceived that a shade came over his brow.

"Do you know the colonel?" she asked.

"I never saw him before yesterday. I appear to have given him some offence—certainly most unintentionally on my part. But he seems to have conceived a strange antipathy to me, and has caused my dismissal from Hazlemere. Till he appeared, I experienced nothing but kindness from Mr. Radcliffe and every inmate in the house."

"And you cannot account for his dislike of you?"

"Perhaps I can—but I cannot very easily explain it. To speak frankly, it is to avoid meeting him again that I desire not to remain longer here."

"Have you practised as an artist in London, Mr. St. Ives?" she inquired, after a pause. "Perhaps you are a student of the Royal Academy?"

"No, I have not that distinction," he rejoined. "I have but lately returned from Paris, where the first essays in my profession were made, and it is possible I may go back there. If your ladyship cares to know my history, you can learn it from Mrs. Radcliffe."

"I shall learn very little from her," she rejoined, smiling. "To tell you the truth, I have already made the attempt."

"Mrs. Radcliffe acted wisely," he observed, with a melancholy smile. "There is nothing to interest you. My history will best be told some ten years hence."

"Ten years hence! that's a long time. We shall all be grown old then. You expect to become famous—eh?"

"I aspire to win reputation as a portrait painter."

"A future Sir Joshua—eh?"

"I hope some day to have the honour of painting your ladyship's portrait. Sir Joshua himself could not have desired a better subject."

"I shall be delighted to give you a sitting," said her ladyship, with a well-pleased smile. "But I can't wait ten years. I shall have lost my good looks before that."

"You shall not wait ten minutes, if you will allow me to sketch you. I succeeded tolerably well with Miss Radcliffe yesterday, and I may be as fortunate with your ladyship."

"So you have taken May! She has never

shown me your performance. I should like to
have Azo taken of all things. Try what you can
make of us."

Hilary immediately opened his portfolio, and
prepared for the task.

Moving her horse to a little distance, her ladyship took up a position.

" Will that do?" she asked.

The artist nodded approval.

"Stand still, Azo," she cried, smoothing her
steed's silken mane with the handle of her whip.
" My pet is going to have his picture taken."

And as if he understood what was required of
him, Azo remained tolerably quiet.

Hilary, as we know, worked with great rapidity.
But he had more to do now than on the previous
occasion. However, he got through his task with
surprising expedition, and succeeded in making a
most spirited sketch.

Her ladyship was enchanted. Praise to a young

artist is delicious, but praise from such lips as
Myrtilla's is indescribably sweet.

"Landseer could not have done better," she
cried, enthusiastically. "My pet Azo is drawn
to the life. I must have this sketch, Mr. St.
Ives. Ask anything you please for it—*anything.*"

"I will only ask you to accept it," he rejoined,
blushing with pleasure.

"Nay, I really cannot——"

"Since I must have some reward, give me this
glove."

She had dropped it, while examining the sketch.

"Upon my word, you are a proficient in
gallantry as well as art," cried her ladyship,
smiling.

"I shall keep it as a souvenir of Boxgrove," he
cried, placing the glove within his breast.

The refined gallantry of his manner was not lost
upon her.

" Decidedly, he is no common person," she thought.

With one of her most captivating smiles, she then asked him if he would like to see the house, adding, that she would have great pleasure in showing it to him.

"I know how much I shall lose in declining your ladyship's tempting offer," he replied. "But I cannot run the risk of meeting any of the party from Hazlemere."

"Don't be alarmed on that account. None of them will be here for an hour or two."

"I am compelled to differ with your ladyship. Unless I am greatly mistaken, yonder is Colonel Delacombe," said Hilary, pointing out a cavalier who had just entered the park, and was evidently shaping his course towards the mansion.

"You are right. 'Tis he!" she exclaimed.

"I have the honour to wish your ladyship good day."

"Why beat a retreat?" she cried. "Are you afraid of him?"

"Afraid! no!" exclaimed Hilary, proudly. "Colonel Delacombe has more reason than I have to avoid the meeting."

"Then stay and face him. Ha! he sees us. He is galloping in this direction."

It was now a point of honour with Hilary to remain.

Shortly afterwards the colonel came up, his looks proclaiming surprise and displeasure at the sight of her ladyship's companion.

Saluting her with his accustomed grace, he turned to Hilary, and said, sharply,

"You here, sir!"

Myrtilla instantly interposed.

"Visit your displeasure upon me," she said. "I am the offender. Mr. St. Ives has remained here at my request."

"He should not have come here at all," rejoined the colonel. "He would have shown better taste by leaving the neighbourhood. I would recommend his prompt departure."

Myrtilla again tried to interpose, but ineffectually.

Hilary's face flushed deeply. He met the colonel's look with a glance as stern as his own.

"I must ask Colonel Delacombe by what right he presumes to question my taste, or to give me advice?" he said.

"It must suffice that I have expressed my opinion, sir," rejoined the colonel, haughtily.

"Pardon me, sir, that will not suffice," rejoined Hilary, boldly. "Why are you surprised to find me here? Why do you complain of my remaining in the neighbourhood? Above all, why do you enjoin my departure?"

"What have you to say to all this, colonel?"

asked Myrtilla, who, it must be confessed, rather enjoyed his confusion. "If Mr. St. Ives has offended you, I am sure he will be ready to apologise."

"Your ladyship is very good to undertake his defence, but I bring no charge against him. I simply expressed surprise at seeing him here after the manner in which he had quitted Hazlemere."

"What manner?" cried Hilary, indignantly. "I left Hazlemere chiefly because I was given to understand by Mr. Radcliffe and Mr. Thornton that my presence—from some cause or other which you can best explain—is disagreeable to you. So far I have obeyed you. But I refuse to obey your mandate now, unless you can show that you have some right to exact obedience from me."

"Have you such right, colonel?" cried Myrtilla, laughing.

"I appeal to Mr. St. Ives's good taste and

good feeling," said the colonel. "I hope he will see the impropriety of remaining in this neighbourhood—especially after his own expressed determination — and I think a little reflection will convince him that I am right."

"You are right, sir," replied Hilary. "I confess that I have acted inconsiderately, and inconsistently with my own professions. I will go at once."

And bowing to her ladyship, who sought by a look to restrain him, he departed.

"Upon my word, colonel, you have dealt harshly with the young man," said her ladyship, in a reproachful tone.

"I am compelled to act thus. Don't ask for an explanation. I cannot give it."

"Well, look at this drawing. Pretty—ain't it? Own that our young artist must be uncommonly clever to make such a sketch as this off-hand. I won't say anything about myself — though I think I come out tolerably well—but my pet Azo is perfection."

"Azo and his mistress are both excellently done," said the colonel. "The fellow has undoubted talent."

"I like the sketch so much that I mean to have it framed, and hang it up in my boudoir."

"I was in hopes you were going to give it me. Won't you?"

"No, thank you. If you want a copy, apply to the artist. I don't mean to part with it. What do you think I gave for it?"

"Can't say. It would be cheap at a guinea."

"You shouldn't have it for twenty. The gallant young artist would take no other payment than one of my gloves."

"And you gave him your glove?" cried the colonel, frowning.

" Where was the harm? I thought it a romantic idea. Come, let us take a canter."

Away they went together at a swift pace down a long, sweeping glade, disturbing the deer, and then more slowly up the hill-side. By this time the colonel had recovered his temper, but he did not press his suit with the same ardour as heretofore. For nearly an hour they continued riding about the park, admiring its beauties, and the extensive views it commanded. But they saw nothing more of poor Hilary.

They then proceeded to the stables, where they remained until the arrival of the whole party from Hazlemere. Much to the colonel's relief, Mrs. Sutton did not accompany her mistress on this occasion. Lady Richborough, who was extremely proud of the sketch, took care it should be seen by everybody, and, of course, it was generally admired. But no one, except Sir Charles, made any inquiries about the artist. Curious to know what had passed between Hilary and the colonel, Mrs. Radcliffe questioned her ladyship in private, and after hearing the details of the interview, she could not help remarking, " I think the colonel behaves very badly to the young man."

"I gave him a hint to that effect," said her ladyship. " Pray what has Mr. St. Ives done to offend the colonel?"

" First, he was unlucky enough to be brought to Hazlemere. But that was not the poor fellow's own fault. I fear the colonel will never forgive him."

" But why need he care for the colonel's forgiveness? What is the colonel to him; or he to the colonel?"

" Don't ask me to give an opinion on that point."

"Well, all I can say is, that he would quite cut the colonel out in a drawing-room. I am sorry he is gone."

The interval between luncheon and dinner was spent in billiards and croquet. In the latter pleasant game Sir Charles was an expert, and luckily May was equally fond of it, and played equally well, so they were capitally matched.

A croquet party, on a smooth lawn, with a tent close at hand, and a fine old mansion in the back-ground, forms a pretty picture; and when two such charming personages as May and Myrtilla figure among the players, the picture is prettier still. Both Sir Charles and Oswald were quite sorry when it was time to dress for dinner. Colonel Delacombe had never played at croquet before, but he profited by the instructions given him by her ladyship.

Sir Charles's cook being a cordon bleu the

dinner was perfect. Mr. Dancer had special
orders about the wine, and took particular care
of Mr. Radcliffe and Mr. Thornton. Old Madeira
and a bottle of Marshal Soult's sherry at dinner,
with a magnum of Laffitte after, made them both
superlatively happy.

After a little music, the whole party adjourned
to the billiard-room to witness a match between
Lady Richborough and the colonel, in which her
ladyship came off the victor. Apparently, the
colonel had quite forgotten the annoying incident of the morning, and seemed just as much
enamoured as before.

To Sir Charles the day had been one of unin-
terrupted bliss.

XII.

THE INTERVIEW IN TRAFALGAR-SQUARE.

ALL went smoothly with the lovers. The skies were bright above them—their path was strewn with flowers. Not a quarrel has to be recorded. No untoward or unlooked-for event marred their happiness.

Sir Charles's love amounted to idolatry. Never happy, except in May's society—he was constantly by her side. Whether she was in the charming gardens of Hazlemere—at work in the drawing-room—on horseback in the shady lanes, or on the breezy common—whether she paced the stately terrace at Boxgrove—strolled forth into the park—or loitered amid the woods to admire the deer—Sir Charles was near her.

Sometimes, Myrtilla was with them—but not always. They were so wrapped up in each other, that they had not a thought for her. She voted them both intensely stupid, and told them so. They only laughed, and gave small heed to what she said.

Ah! those were halcyon days. If such days would last, this earth would indeed be paradise.

But let us not disturb their happiness by any gloomy anticipations of the future. Fortunately for themselves, lovers never look beyond the present hour. Love is eternal, they believe, and will withstand the rudest shock. Dream on, then, happy pair! We will not disturb you, or chase away your visions of delight.

Nearly a month passed away thus blissfully. Early and late, May and her lover were together. Neither had a plan with which the other was not connected. Each day, in Myrtilla's estimation, they grew more stupid than they had been the day before. She had no patience with Charlie, and would no longer listen to his rhapsodies. Impossible to live with them, if they went on in this manner. However, she consoled herself by thinking that they must soon come to their senses, since it was arranged that the marriage should take place early in July.

Sir Charles's engagement was vexatious to her ladyship in one respect. It detained her at Boxgrove longer than she liked. Her house in Eaton-place was prepared for her. The season had commenced. Lots of parties were going on—dinners, balls, fancy balls, musical soirées. Every post brought her cards of invitation, and notes from the nicest people imaginable, telling her she was sadly missed, and imploring her to come up to town without delay.

These notes drove her wild. She longed to be seen in the Park, where a host of admirers were on the look-out for her daily. She longed for the box at the Opera, with which Sir Charles had heretofore indulged her. She longed to see the Derby run, but that she knew to be impossible. However, she made up her mind to go to Ascot. She thought Boxgrove the dullest place on earth. Never had the gardens and the park looked more exquisite. But what did she care for the gardens and the park when everybody was in town! She very much preferred Kensington Gardens and Hyde Park. She had promised Charlie to stay, and stay she would, if he insisted. But why not let her take May to Eaton-place? May had never yet had a season in town, and would enjoy a few weeks' gaiety immensely. She ought to go out a little before her marriage. Improvement was scarcely possible, but a month in town would give her the last finish.

Sir Charles shook his head, and entreated her not to mention the subject to May. So far from improving her, a month in town would take off the freshness which was so charming to him, and which, like the down on the peach, could never be restored.

Myrtilla laughed at his objections, and told him he was a selfish fellow, and wanted to keep May all to himself, but she promised compliance.

In spite, however, of her brother's interdiction, she *did* propose the plan to May, and held out so many inducements that, as she expected, the young girl was quite dazzled. On being consulted, Mrs. Radcliffe gave her assent, and could see nothing but what was delightful in the arrangement. Just the thing for May.

Unable to offer a remonstrance, Sir Charles

reluctantly acquiesced. If he had a presentiment of ill, he kept it to himself.

So it was settled that her ladyship and May were to go up to Eaton-place, and arrangements were made accordingly.

Where was Colonel Delacombe all this while? Had he been rejected by Myrtilla, or given up all idea of her? Neither one nor the other. He was just as much enamoured as ever, but had not yet proposed. His visit to Hazlemere did not extend beyond the third day, when his attendance being required at the Horse Guards, he hastened up to town. He had accepted an invitation to Boxgrove, but was obliged to postpone it. At least, he pleaded a variety of unavoidable engagements. Mrs. Radcliffe also was very urgent for his return to Hazlemere. But he made the same excuses to her.

In fact, he was trying, though ineffectually, as

it turned out, to conquer his passion for the fascinating Myrtilla.

Now that the colonel was gone, her ladyship, by
way of amusing herself, would not have been indisposed to renew her flirtation with Oswald; but
that disconsolate young fellow did not give her the
opportunity, but started off rather suddenly for
Bowdon, in Cheshire, where, it may be remem-
bered, his mother resided, in order to obtain some
solace under his bitter disappointment.

Mr. Thornton, however, was still at Hazlemere,
and since a younger man was not to be had, her
ladyship diverted herself by an occasional flirtation
with him. The old gentleman was almost beside
himself. No fool like an old fool.

Recent events had disturbed the calm tenor of
Mrs. Radcliffe's existence, and she could not re-
gain her tranquillity. The colonel had promised
to return immediately, but, as before mentioned,

he did not keep his word. He wrote her a short apologetic note, the cold and distant tone of which she did not like at all. He was still at the Langham, and seemed well pleased with his quarters. Mr. Thornton, at his daughter's request, ran up to see him, but did not succeed in bringing him back.

Mrs. Sutton, too, was greatly changed. Her deportment was different from what it used to be, and at times she scarcely attempted to conceal the aversion she entertained for her mistress. Evidently, she could not forget the humiliation she had experienced from Colonel Delacombe. She could not endure to hear his name mentioned, and rudely checked her mistress whenever she alluded to him.

The housekeeper, however, manifested no reluctance to talk about Hilary St. Ives. Indeed, she often spoke of him, and with a tenderness and affection that surprised Mrs. Radcliffe. For reasons that need not be explained, she at once took possession of the five hundred pounds, and caused the clothes-chest, with all its contents, to be removed to her own chamber.

Had Mrs. Radcliffe seen her when she was alone that night, or overheard some ejaculations that escaped her, she would have been terrified. The expression of her countenance showed that she was under the empire of the worst passions.

All her machinations had come to naught. She had foolishly persuaded herself that by her influence over Mrs. Radcliffe, and the arts she intended to employ with May, she could contrive to bring about a union between the fair young damsel and Hilary. This scheme, though promising at first, proved abortive. May was quickly snatched from her grasp. Then Colonel Delacombe thwarted the remainder of her designs.

She hated him—but while hating him, she feared him. We have seen that she shrank before his glance, and that her rage was impotent against him. All these things occupied her when she was alone that night in her chamber, and gave her countenance an almost fiendish expression.

Yet amidst the storm that agitated her, there were intervals of calm—amid the darkness occasional gleams of light. Her mood instantly changed when she thought of Hilary. Though he had bestowed the affection which she felt to be her due upon one who had no claim to it, and whom she herself detested, she felt no anger against him on that account. He had pained and grieved her, but she forgave him. Her sole anxiety was for his welfare. She would sacrifice her life to serve him.

But these gentler feelings were not of long duration. Evil passions gained the mastery, and lashed her into fresh fury. Revenge was in her power—terrible revenge !—and she would have it. But the fitting moment for the execution of her dark design had not yet arrived. She could wait. Her victims could not escape her. Neither should she swerve from her purpose.

Revenge was her last thought that night. Revenge her first thought on the morrow.

But while she nourished these vindictive designs, she continued to play her accustomed part as well as her fierce temper would permit. She did not always wear the mask of servility, as we have said, in Mrs. Radcliffe's presence, but at other times she was submissive enough, and she was more than usually attentive to Mr. Radcliffe.

At Mrs. Radcliffe's request she endeavoured to trace out Hilary. She easily ascertained that he stayed for two days at a small inn adjoining

Boxgrove Park, after which he started on foot for London. She heard of him at Ashtead, and learnt that he had crossed Wimbledon Common, but what became of him afterwards she could not discover. As well look for a needle in a bottle of hay as try to find him in mighty London. Yet she made the attempt.

An idea had occurred to her. The Exhibition of the Royal Academy was then open, and Hilary's tastes as an artist might not improbably take him there. Slender as was the chance of meeting him, it ought not to be neglected. Accordingly she went to the Exhibition, and spent nearly two hours in wandering through the rooms, and examining—not the pictures—but the groups collected before them. Nowhere could she discover him.

Just as she was about to abandon her search, he entered one of the larger rooms. His lofty figure did not allow her to lose sight of him. After a struggle with the throng, she reached him. He was planted before a noble picture by Maclise, and was studying it so intently, that he did not perceive her. She touched his arm, and, as he turned, his looks betokened the greatest surprise.

Perhaps he would have avoided her, if he could —at least, such was her impression. But he did not refuse to attend her.

Quitting the picture galleries, they crossed the street and descended to the spacious inclosure of the square, where the fountains are wont to play, and where, comparatively speaking, they were alone.

As they paced to and fro, Mrs. Sutton commenced by expressing her great satisfaction at meeting with him, admitting that she had been in quest of him, and after chiding him for his sudden flight from Hazlemere, told him in the kindest terms she could employ, that she was still most anxious to serve him, and fondly hoped he would not decline her assistance.

"Do not think me ungrateful for the kindness you have shown me," he rejoined, "or for the interest you still take in me, but——"

"You are too proud to place yourself under an obligation to me. But a time may come when you may be less scrupulous. Pray let me know how I can communicate with you?"

He hesitated, but at last said,

"You must excuse me. I have reasons for withholding my address."

"You believe that I am acting for others. You are wrong. I am personally interested in you—personally, I repeat. Do not disregard my friendship. I have the power and the will to serve you. In proof, let me tell you that it was

I who sent the money and the clothes which you
supposed came from Colonel Delacombe."

"Then the letter I received was written by
you?" he cried, in astonishment.

"It was. I adopted that roundabout course
because I thought it would be most agreeable to
your feelings. You will understand my motives
better one of these days. Have I said enough
to remove your scruples? I have the money
with me, and entreat your acceptance of it—as a
gift—as a loan."

"I can only accept it on the condition of your
giving me a full explanation of this seeming
mystery. What am I to you that you take such
interest in me?"

"What are you to me?" she cried, stopping,
and regarding him with inexpressible tenderness.

She seemed about to pour forth the secrets of
her heart, but suddenly checking herself, she

added, "No—no—you must not ask me why I act thus. I cannot tell you."

"You have said too much," he exclaimed. "I have a right to further explanation."

But Mrs. Sutton's momentary weakness had passed.

"Be content with what you have learnt. Will you take the money?"

Hilary shook his head.

"I know from whom it comes," he rejoined. "You are employed by Mrs. Radcliffe. You act your part admirably. But you cannot impose upon me."

This was too much. Mrs. Sutton struggled hard with herself, but could not repress an outburst of emotion.

"You do me a great injustice," she ejaculated, in a broken voice. "But I forgive you. Farewell."

"Stay," he cried, detaining her. " Do not quit me in anger."

"In anger!" she exclaimed. "If you could read my heart you would find no anger there— but much grief."

Just then an elderly man descended the broad stone steps leading from the street, and walked slowly towards them. He had been watching them for some minutes from above, without attracting their attention. He was high-shouldered, and from his halting gait appeared to be lame. Though respectably dressed in black, he had not altogether the air of a gentleman.

" Who is that coming towards us?" cried Mrs. Sutton. "He seems to know you."

"Mr. Courtenay, of Exeter," replied Hilary "He was to meet me at the Exhibition. I suppose he has seen me talking with you."

"Is that Mr. Courtenay?" she exclaimed, in

alarm. "I must begone. For Heaven's sake do not tell him who I am. Write to me—write to me, I beseech you, if you have any love for me. Attend to my caution. Farewell!"

And regardless of the construction that might be put upon her conduct, she hurried off to the lower part of the square.

XIII.

MAY'S FIRST BALL IN TOWN.

ON her return to Hazlemere, Mrs. Sutton informed her mistress of her meeting with Hilary at the Exhibition, but she gave no details of the interview, merely stating that he had refused all offers of assistance, and had declined to acquaint her with his address. She made no mention whatever of Mr. Courtenay.

Mrs. Sutton was not without hope that Hilary would comply with her parting request, and was sorely disappointed when no letter came from him.

Mrs. Radcliffe could no longer share her griefs with the housekeeper. Vexed at the colonel's prolonged absence, she addressed two or three reproachful letters to him, begging him to come down instantly—if only for a day—and if this was absolutely impossible, entreating him to send her a few lines calculated to dissipate the dreadful ennui under which she laboured. To her infinite annoyance, these letters remained unanswered. It did not occur to her that they had never been posted.

The result of all this worry upon Mrs. Radcliffe was to rouse her in some degree from her indolent habits. One morning, to her husband's great surprise, she announced that she should like to spend a few weeks in town. She wished to be on the spot—to see how things went on in Eaton-place.

May was inexperienced, and a little judicious maternal advice might now and then be necessary. Lady Richborough was everything that could be desired as a chaperon, but occasions might arise when an older head would be useful. Feeling this, and ready to make any sacrifice for her child, she had resolved to go to town, not for the purpose of interfering with Lady Richborough's arrangements, or going out with her ladyship and May, but simply with the design of watching over the dear child, and seeing that all went on properly.

Mr. Radcliffe entirely approved of the plan, and so did Mr. Thornton, who was present at the time. They fully appreciated the sacrifice of her own inclinations which they felt she was making.

Apart, however, from any other considerations, Mr. Radcliffe told her that the change could not fail to be beneficial to herself, while he hoped and believed she would enjoy a short visit to town when the season was at its height, whether she mixed with society or not.

Next day the two old gentlemen went up to town, and, with the assistance of Colonel Dela-combe, whom they called upon, were fortunately enabled to secure a very charming house in Upper Brook-street.

The colonel sent a message to Mrs. Radcliffe to say that he was enchanted by her determination, and hoped she would like the house he had been instrumental in choosing for her. He appeared to be overwhelmed by engagements. This might, perhaps, account for his inexplicable silence. Mrs. Radcliffe was willing to believe so, and quite re-covered her spirits.

Mrs. Sutton was pleased with the arrangement. It suited her plans.

But May was greatly surprised by it. That mamma, who had never left home for years, and who had often declared that nothing should induce her to leave home again, should propose a visit to town, seemed the most unlikely thing possible. But unlikely things are just the things that always happen, as Myrtilla told her. Of course May was delighted. Myrtilla *said* she was delighted. And Sir Charles really *was* delighted. On all accounts, it rejoiced him that the family were going up to town.

May's début in fashionable society took place on the very night of her arrival in town, at Lady Oldcastle's ball at Prince's-gate, and created an extraordinary sensation. Everybody admitted that she was by far the loveliest girl that the season had as yet produced, and it did not seem at all likely that she could be eclipsed. Such charming features—such a delicately fair complexion—such soft blue eyes—such superb blonde tresses—and such an exquisite figure had never been seen

before. And then she looked so fresh and un·
sophisticated—so full of natural enjoyment—that
twenty blasé young fellows, proof against ordinary
attractions, were smitten at first sight, and driven
to despair when they learnt she was already
engaged. All eyes followed her as she moved
through the rooms, and though there was some
disposition to criticise her among mammas and ·
chaperons jealous of their daughters' and charges'
beauty, no real fault could be found with her.
The worst that could be said was, that she was
not quite accustomed to society. However, since
no rivalry was to be expected from her, envy was
silenced, and her surpassing loveliness universally
admitted. Had she been in the market, the judgment pronounced upon her would have been very
different. Her movements in the dance were so
graceful that she caused a perfect fureur, and
there was a host of aspirants for the honour of

her hand. She liked dancing, and danced a good deal—almost every dance, we are afraid to say—and had the best partners in the room.

" You will fatigue yourself to death, my love," observed Lady Richborough. " You should follow my example, and never exceed a couple of valses. Recollect that you have three balls to-morrow night."

May was about to follow the advice, but her partner, who was no other than Captain de Vesci, Colonel Delacombe's friend, looked so blank and disappointed, that she took compassion upon him, and was instantly involved in the mazy ring.

" Lucky Sir Charles is not here," remarked her ladyship to Colonel Delacombe, who was seated beside her on a sofa in one of the smaller rooms. " I wonder what he would say to all this ?"

" He would be charmed, of course, to see the object of his choice so much admired."

"I'm not so sure of that," said her ladyship, smiling. "Sir Charles is of a remarkably jealous nature. If he could have his own way, I don't think he would let May go out at all."

"You amaze me!" cried the colonel. "I fancied he knew your sex better, and had more reliance on himself. Why should a woman, who is calculated to shine in society, be excluded from it? The plan never answers. I have known several young married people, who thought they could live for themselves alone, and were foolish enough to try the experiment. What was the result? Most of them, if not all, are now separated. If you want a woman to run away from you, shut her up. That's an infallible maxim. For my part," he continued, looking earnestly at her, in order to give due force to his words, "nothing would delight me so much as to see my wife admired. I should feel myself flattered by the compliments paid her."

"But how can you tell, colonel, since you have never been married?" observed her ladyship, archly.

"I can't speak practically. But I know myself sufficiently to be certain as to how I should be affected under such circumstances. Homage to my wife I should regard as homage to myself. If her charms and accomplishments excited admiration, I should feel proud of her, not jealous. Other people may covet the treasure I possess, but that would only make me value it the more. If we have a priceless gem, we do not hide it, but allow it to be seen, and the admiration it excites is in the highest degree gratifying to us. Such would be my conduct towards my wife—if I had one." And he again looked at her ladyship expressively.

"Your notions are strictly orthodox, colonel, and meet my entire approval," rejoined her ladyship. "I wonder you do not give effect to them."

"I have no chance of doing so. I am too fastidious to choose any other than a young and handsome woman, and such a woman would not be likely to accept an old scarred soldier like myself, while plenty of good-looking young fellows are to be had. I ought to have married long ago, but I have had no time to look out for a wife, and in India there is but little choice."

"I am surprised at that. I should have thought just the contrary. But what prevents you from choosing now? There are pretty girls in abundance here."

"A pretty girl would not suit me. I must have something brilliant."

"A jewel such as you described just now?"

"Exactly."

"That is not so easily found. Diamonds are not to be met with every day."

"I have been singularly fortunate," said the colonel. "I have discovered one of inestimable worth."

Her ladyship was quite fluttered. She could not affect to misunderstand him.

But before anything more could be said by the colonel, a very unseasonable interruption was offered by a handsome, though rather effeminate-looking young man, with a pale complexion and light flowing whiskers, who begged her ladyship, in drawling tones, to present him to Miss Radcliffe.

"Charming creature!" he cried. "Should like immensely to valse with her."

"No chance to-night, dear Lord Robert," she rejoined. "I know she's engaged four or five deep."

"Deuced unlucky that! Will your ladyship give me a galoppe?"

"Don't ask me, please. I'm tired. Besides, I want to take Miss Radcliffe away if I can."

"What, so early! and before she has fulfilled her engagements!" cried Lord Robert Tadcaster. "I must protest against such cruelty. Ah, here she comes!"

As he spoke May was brought back by Captain de Vesci. Lord Robert was presented, but May was unable to dance with him for the reasons assigned by Lady Richborough.

"Have you had enough, my love?" said her ladyship. "Recollect you are on your good behaviour to-night. Sir Charles will never forgive me if I allow you to remain out late."

"I am quite ready to go," said May. "But unluckily——"

"Never mind your engagements. They don't signify in the least. Lord Robert will give you his arm."

Attended by the colonel, and followed by May and the young nobleman, her ladyship then quitted the ball-room without taking leave of Lady Oldcastle.

Lady Richborough's box at the Opera was the general resort of the golden youth of the day. It was full of them. Driven to the pit or to some other box, Sir Charles had the annoyance of witnessing the attentions paid his fiancée by a succession of impertinent coxcombs.

How often he wished himself back at Box-grove! and how firmly he resolved that May should never have an opera-box.

But this was the slightest of his grievances. The same set of coxcombs who beset Lady Rich-borough's opera-box met her ladyship and May —as if by appointment—during their morning ride in Hyde Park, and would not be dismissed. They did not care for Sir Charles's black looks. Chief among these pests were Lord Robert Tad-caster and Captain de Vesci. Sometimes, Sir

Charles was exasperated to such a degree by their impertinences that he would have affronted them but for the interference of Colonel Delacombe.

The colonel, who was now recognised by Sir Charles as his sister's suitor, always attended her ladyship during her promenades, and indeed was generally with her in the evening as well as during the morning.

Seeing, or fancying they saw, how matters stood, people invited him to all the parties to which her ladyship was bidden. The colonel, therefore, was in immense request, and became extremely and deservedly popular. Attentions paid to her ladyship never put him out. He resigned his seat by her side without a murmur, or fell back if a gay cavalier, whose chat he knew would amuse her, wanted to join her in Rotten-row. Thus it will be seen that he acted up to his own precepts, and would fain have instilled them into Sir Charles.

" Jealousy is an absurd passion," he said, " and
always makes the person who yields to it ridiculous. Even if I were fool enough to be
jealous, I would take good care not to let my
wife perceive it. A woman always despises a
jealous husband, and not unfrequently ends by
giving him real ground for jealousy. Take my
advice, and do not give yourself the slightest
concern about these imbeciles. May is totally
indifferent to them. She is amused by their
bavardage, no doubt, but she rates them at their
real worth. Do not make them of importance by
quarrelling with any of them. Treat them as a
pack of fools, and laugh at them as I do."

Very sensible advice. But Sir Charles could
not follow it. He had many a severe trial to
undergo, but one of the worst was at Ascot.

XIV.

LADY RICHBOROUGH, as we are aware, had resolved to go to Ascot. Sir Charles objected, but his objections were quickly overruled. The colonel, who had become a sort of Mentor to him, counselled him to give way with a good grace, and he did so. May said it was so kind of him. She longed, of all things, to go to Ascot, of which she had heard so much. New dresses were ordered—new bonnets—and all preparations made.

Mrs. Radcliffe no sooner heard of the plan than she determined to join the party. She had not witnessed a race for upwards of twenty years. At any risk she must go. So *she* ordered new dresses and new bonnets.

The party was further increased by Oswald and his mother, who had just come to town. Of the latter we must say a word. Mrs. Woodcot was not so handsome as her sister, but had very pleasing features, fine eyes, a very good figure, and very agreeable manners. Very well dressed, too, for a country lady.

Sir Charles made all necessary arrangements. He engaged rooms at the Castle Hotel, Windsor, for the whole party, which of course comprised the colonel and Mr. Thornton. Open carriages were at their disposal, and in these they drove daily through the park to the racecourse. The weather being luckily propitious, nothing could be more enjoyable.

At all times the drive through this magnificent park is delightful, but in Ascot time it is peculiarly exhilarating. Every turn-out looks well. Teams bowl along merrily. Postilions appear conscious of their own importance. Everybody is well dressed and in high spirits.

Our friends were capitally turned out. Four splendid horses attached to each carriage bore them along gallantly. Lady Richborough and May, attended by Sir Charles and the colonel, occupied the first carriage. Both ladies looked ravishingly beautiful in their charming summer toilettes. May was full of excitement and delight — perfectly enchanted by the novel scene.

But the comparative quietude of the forest, with its long avenues, its grand old trees, and stretching glades, was soon exchanged for the crowd, confusion, and bewildering noises of the racecourse. What stoppages! what vociferations!

what strange-looking people! But what excitement!

Mrs. Radcliffe, who came in the second carriage with Mrs. Woodcot, was quite terrified, half-screamed at every turn, and felt certain she should be upset. But both carriages got safely into the place reserved for them, which was the best place possible, being just opposite the Grand Stand. Then the poor lady could now look about her with comfort, and survey the surprising scene. She owned that it far surpassed all her preconceived notions. And if she was astonished, what wonder that her daughter, to whom such a spectacle was an absolute novelty, should be greatly excited!

London had sent forth all its flower of fashion to the course. It had sent forth multitudes of others who had no pretension to rank or fashion, but still the aristocratic element was clearly perceptible in the crowd.

London had likewise sent forth all its beauty
—or the best part of it. Hundreds of lovely
women were to be seen in the long lines of carriages drawn up near the ropes. Hundreds of
others, equally lovely, could be observed on the
lawn and on the seats of the Grand Stand, looking in their gay attire, and with their wonder-
fully-varied parasols, like a vast parterre of
flowers. But we unhesitatingly declare, that none
so lovely could be discerned, either in the Grand
Stand or elsewhere, as in the carriage containing
Lady Richborough and May. This was proved
by the universal admiration they excited.

To this sort of admiration Sir Charles could
not object, and he was rather gratified by it—
but he was very soon put out of humour.

The same set of coxcombs who had been his
bane in Rotten-row, at the Opera, and at many
an evening party, speedily discovered the car-

riage, and invaded it. There they were monopo-
lising May, laughing, jesting in the most imper-
tinently familiar manner, talking about the horses,
and offering bets of gloves.

In order to get rid of his tormentors, Sir Charles
proposed that the ladies should go over to the
Grand Stand, and take possession of their box.
Agreed to. But the plaguy fellows were not to be
shaken off. Lord Robert Tadcaster immediately
offered his arm to May, and De Vesci insisted
upon escorting Myrtilla.

" Confound their impertinence ! " cried Sir
Charles. " I can't stand it any longer."

" It is a bore," rejoined the colonel. " But
pray keep quiet."

We shall pass by what happened in the Grand
Stand. Sir Charles's temper was certainly not
improved. After the race for the Gold Cup had
been run, they returned to the carriage for

luncheon, and the same sort of thing occurred again—a degree worse, perhaps. Sir Charles and the colonel were both excluded from the carriage, and their seats occupied by the odious De Vesci, and the still more odious Lord Robert, who laughed and chatted with the ladies, while they quaffed the iced champagne and helped to demolish the lobster salad and pigeon pie. Sir Charles was so disgusted that he went to have luncheon with Mrs. Radcliffe, and the colonel went with him.

They had not been gone many minutes when a very tawny, but handsome gipsy made her way to the carriage, and fixing her black eyes on May, addressed her in the customary formula,

" Let me tell you your fortune, my pretty young lady."

" Yes, do let her tell it you, Miss Radcliffe," cried Lord Robert, slipping a sovereign into the gipsy's hand. "I long so much to hear it. I wonder whether she'll tell it right."

"My words will come true for sartin," rejoined the gipsy, confidently. "But no one but the young lady must hear 'em. Let me look at your hand, my pretty lady."

After a moment's inspection of May's white palm, she whispered in the young lady's ear, "Look over my shoulder, my dear—look straight afore you."

May complied, and perceived amidst the crowd, on the further side of the ropes, a tall young man, who was watching the scene. She could not mistake him. It was Hilary St. Ives.

"That's him as you are to marry," said the gipsy, in the same low tone as before.

XV.

MRS. SUTTON'S INTERVIEW WITH LADY RICHBOROUGH.

AFTER uttering her strange prediction, the gipsy hurried away, refusing to satisfy Lord Robert's curiosity, which was greatly excited by May's blushes and confusion. The cunning fortune-teller had spoken in so low a tone that he could not catch a word she said.

When May looked up again, Hilary had disappeared, and she saw no more of him during the day.

Though quite as curious as Lord Robert to

learn what had occurred, Lady Richborough made
no remark at the time, but when she and May
were alone together in the evening, she questioned
her on the subject, and laughed heartily at the
explanation.

"Oh! that is all," she exclaimed. "I fancied
the gipsy had promised you to Lord Robert, for
I saw him bribe her, but I suppose she was better
paid by Hilary St. Ives. So you are to marry
him, eh? I wouldn't give much for his chance,
notwithstanding the prophecy."

"Nor I. But you must own it is a strange
circumstance," observed May.

"Not so strange as it appears. The gipsy was
in league with Hilary, who told her what to say,
and placed himself where he could be readily
descried. I am glad you did not mention the
matter to Sir Charles. It would only have put
him out."

" Poor fellow! I fear he was greatly put out before that. Dearest Myrtilla, I cannot persevere in the part you have forced me to play, now that I find how much it pains him. Do give that tiresome Lord Robert a hint, or allow me to do so."

"Not yet, my love—not yet, or you will defeat my plan. Sir Charles must and shall be cured of his jealousy."

"But is this the way to cure him? I constantly expect to see him break out into a furious passion."

" Just what I want," said her ladyship, smiling. " Then we will make him heartily ashamed of himself, and his cure will be accomplished."

" But if he is no longer jealous, I shall think he no longer loves me."

" My dear child, it is a mistake to suppose that a jealous man is the most devoted. He is simply intensely selfish and exacting. Sir Charles entertains the preposterous notion, of which I intend to disabuse him, that he is to have you all to himself. Were he allowed his own way, he would exclude you altogether from society, and shut you up at Boxgrove, where you would be as dull as if you were immured in a convent."

"It would be no punishment to me to be shut up, as you term it, at Boxgrove. Indeed, I should prefer it to the rackety life I am now leading. You will laugh at me, I know, Myrtilla, but I declare I am not half so happy as I used to be when rambling daily about the park with dear Sir Charles. How things have altered since we came to town! When we ride out together in Rotten-row, Sir Charles's place is immediately taken by some one whom he dislikes. Very often we do not exchange more than half a dozen words during a whole evening. I find it very hard to obey your instructions. Sir Charles, as you know, doesn't dance, and I am sure—though he never says so—that he thinks I dance a great deal too much. My conduct must appear shocking to him, and though you find plenty of excuses for me, I can find none for myself."

"Having put yourself in my hands, you must do as you are bidden. By-and-by, when you understand things better, you will be grateful for my good advice. Mrs. Radcliffe entirely approves of the plan I am pursuing, and is infinitely obliged to me. She sees as plainly as I do that Sir Charles's design is to keep you in the country. Now I won't have such a charming creature buried alive to please him. You are formed for society, and shall not be withdrawn from it with my consent. As May Radcliffe, you are immensely admired, but you will be ten times more admired as Lady Ilminster. I know from experience the effect that a lovely young married woman of a

certain rank can produce. She carries all before
her. Every house worth entering is thrown open
to her. She is queen of every fête, and a hundred soupirants follow in her train."

" A brilliant picture," observed May, smiling.
" But it does not dazzle me. I must repeat that
I am unequal to the part I am playing. I was
really unhappy this morning when Sir Charles
left the carriage, and would have recalled him if I
could. I thought Lord Robert perfectly detest-
able, and wished him at Jericho, or anywhere else,
except Ascot."

" He has been very useful to us in our little
plot," observed her ladyship. " You need not give
yourself the least concern about a butterfly that
can be brushed off at any moment."

They then separated for the night. May was
tired, but sleep did not visit her so soon as it used
to do, when she was better satisfied with herself.

Things went on pretty much as they had done for another fortnight. Morning fêtes, concerts, grand dinners, and grander balls succeeded each other without interruption, and at all these Lady Richborough and May assisted.

Apparently, Sir Charles was more reconciled to his position, and allowed no outward manifestation of annoyance to escape him. In fact, he appeared indifferent — though this was far from being the case. Had he become philosophical? Or had he penetrated his sister's design? Myrtilla triumphantly declared that they had brought him to his senses; but May's uneasiness increased, and she began seriously to apprehend that she had lost his affections.

Meantime, the business arrangements connected with the approaching nuptials had been going on quietly and satisfactorily. Settlements — those dangerous rocks upon which so many fair barks bound for the matrimonial haven have split — offered no difficulties in this case. All was plain sailing. Sir Charles had announced his intention of settling five thousand a year upon his intended, and his estates were to be charged to that amount. Not to be behindhand in liberality, Mr. Radcliffe agreed to settle another five thousand a year upon his daughter. These arrangements were entrusted to Mr. Thornton, who acted as professional adviser to both parties, and declared he had never been more agreeably employed.

When the deeds were completed, and only lacked the necessary signatures, he told May with a chuckle, that she would soon have ten thousand a year. "And a very nice little income you will find it," he added. "Don't forget that you owe it to grandpapa."

As Colonel Delacombe seemed quite at home at Eaton-place, as he was consulted on all matters

by Lady Richborough, and occasionally did the
honours for her, it is not surprising Mrs. Radcliffe should conclude they were engaged, but she
could not get either of them to admit that they
were so. The colonel always laughed when rallied
on the subject, and declared she did him too
much honour. On one point Mrs. Radcliffe was
perfectly satisfied. She could not, she was convinced, have found a better chaperon for her
daughter than Lady Richborough. May's triumphs
delighted her, and recalled the days when she
herself had been universally admired. Moreover,
she entirely agreed with her ladyship that Sir
Charles must be cured of his absurd jealousy. A
different opinion, however, prevailed among the
rest of the family. Mr. Radcliffe and Mr. Thornton thought May's conduct very foolish, and were
both apprehensive lest Sir Charles should break
off the match.

Mrs. Radcliffe, it will be seen, did not enjoy her

visit to town. Under the circumstances, it was impossible she could do so. She had calculated upon the colonel's attentions, and though provoked by his neglect was compelled to dissemble her rage and disappointment. She was also obliged to put on a mask of friendship for Lady Richborough, whom she detested.

Of late, as we know, she had ceased to impart her griefs to Mrs. Sutton, because she met with little sympathy from her; but one day, being greatly exasperated, she could not help observing to the housekeeper that she felt certain the colonel was about to marry Lady Richborough.

"I do not think the marriage will take place," observed Mrs. Sutton, with a singular smile.

"Why not?" demanded Mrs. Radcliffe, curiously.

"I have my own reasons for thinking so," replied the other.

"Whatever your reasons may be, you are

entirely wrong, Sutton," said her mistress. "I
can no longer delude myself with the notion that
Seymour is a model of constancy. He is faith-
less as the rest of his sex. He has contrived to
captivate Lady Richborough, and she has accepted
him."

"Do you only suspect this?" said the housekeeper, looking at her inquiringly; "or are you
sure?"

"I have not questioned her ladyship on the
subject, Sutton, but her manner towards Seymour
satisfies me of the correctness of my surmise.
Perfidious wretch! I could kill him."

"You kill him!" exclaimed the housekeeper,
scornfully. "You have not the courage to do it."

"Well, perhaps I have not," observed Mrs.
Radcliffe. "I have not the resolution of a Spanish
or Italian woman. But I should have no com-
punction in breaking off the match if I had the
power."

The housekeeper smiled bitterly, and said,

"I know a way to prevent it."

Mrs. Radcliffe looked at her incredulously.

"Entreaties are ineffectual with Seymour, I have tried them. He is immovable."

"Wait till I have had an interview with Lady Richborough, and you will then see whether he will persist."

"We must consider before you take this step, Sutton."

"No consideration is required. For Lady Richborough's sake the step *must* be taken, and without delay."

Next morning, at a tolerably early hour, Mrs. Sutton repaired to Eaton-place, and after a little delay was shown into Lady Richborough's dressing-room. Her ladyship had just finished her toilette, and professing to be delighted to see the housekeeper, begged her to be seated.

Without allowing Mrs. Sutton to enter upon

her business, she gave her a very lively description of the balls at which she and May had been present on the previous nights, and would have gone on much longer in the same strain had she not perceived that the housekeeper was becoming impatient. She then stopped suddenly, and said,

"I suppose you bring me some message from dear Mrs. Radcliffe?"

"No. I have taken the liberty of waiting upon your ladyship at this early hour because I have something important—very important to yourself—to communicate."

"Indeed!" exclaimed Lady Richborough, rather alarmed by her manner.

"I must prepare your ladyship for a disagreeable, and perhaps painful piece of intelligence," pursued Mrs. Sutton. "The disclosure I am about to make is calculated to destroy many agreeable illusions, but it cannot be withheld."

"In Heaven's name, what is it? Don't put me on the rack."

"Before entering into any explanation, I must venture to ask your ladyship a question to which I trust you will not refuse me a precise answer. Is there any truth in the report that you are about to be united to Colonel Delacombe?"

"I now see your errand, Sutton," cried her ladyship, laughing. "Though you deny it, I am sure you have been sent by Mrs. Radcliffe to put that question to me."

"Your ladyship is quite mistaken. No one has sent me. No one is aware of my visit. No one will hear of it from me. If you will give me an assurance that an engagement does not subsist between you and Colonel Delacombe nothing more need be said."

"As I cannot exactly give you such an assurance, Sutton, you must assume what you please."

"Then I am bound to tell your ladyship that if such a marriage is contemplated, it can never take place."

Myrtilla turned excessively pale, and after a moment's silence, said,

"What do you mean, Sutton? Is there any serious impediment?"

Laying her hand upon her ladyship's arm, and fixing her eyes full upon her, the housekeeper said in a low voice:

"An insuperable impediment. He is already married."

Myrtilla uttered an exclamation of surprise and anger. Shaking off the housekeeper's grasp, she cried, with great indignation,

"Nonsense, Sutton! I won't believe it. Is it likely that Colonel Delacombe—a man of unquestionable honour—would, if he were married, pay his addresses to a lady, and seek to obtain her hand? I can guess the author of the calumny. Tell her I disbelieve it and despise it."

"Again I must set your ladyship right," rejoined Mrs. Sutton, calmly. "I alone am responsible for the statement, and I affirm its truth."

Her manner carried conviction with it, and frightened Lady Richborough.

"If necessary, I am prepared to substantiate my assertion," continued Mrs. Sutton, after a pause. "But Colonel Delacombe will not dare to deny the accusation."

"We shall see," cried Lady Richborough. "Oh! Sutton, you have made me wretched—most wretched."

"Better your ladyship should suffer now than later on, when the error would be irreparable."

"Yes, if what you say is true, you have indeed saved me from a terrible fate. But since you have said so much, you must tell me all. Where is his wife? What is she? Why has he separated from her?"

"Your ladyship must not question me further," rejoined the housekeeper, in a troubled tone. "I have told you all that is necessary. Thus much I will say. It was a most unlucky union, and attended with sad consequences."

"Has he abandoned his wife?"

"Ask him. Perhaps he may tell you. I cannot. It is a very painful history. Nor should any allusion have been made to it but for present circumstances. My errand is done. I wish your ladyship good morning."

"Stay!" cried Myrtilla, detaining her. "A strange suspicion crosses me. Pray satisfy my doubts."

"I must again refer you to the colonel," rejoined Mrs. Sutton, evasively. "I have nothing more to disclose. You are now in possession of his secret, and can use it as you please."

XVI.

THE COLONEL'S EXPLANATION.

LADY RICHBOROUGH would not see the colonel that day. She feigned sudden indisposition, and kept her own room. Her first idea was to consult with Sir Charles, and leave him to take such steps as he might deem advisable in a matter so delicate, but having still some doubts as to the truth of the housekeeper's statement, she resolved—after long deliberation—to question the colonel herself.

Of course—in consequence of her ladyship's

supposed illness—all the arrangements for the day
had to be given up. The troop of young men who
expected to join the fair equestrians in Rotten-row
were doomed to disappointment. The Opera was
a blank, since the pleasantest box in the house
was empty that night. Lady Fitton had to fill
up two places at her dinner, and Lady Louisa
Legge's ball was deprived of its chief attractions.

Mrs. Radcliffe, who had heard of the housekeeper's visit, called in Eaton-place, and hearing
that her ladyship was indisposed, expressed great
anxiety to see her, but was not admitted to her
room.

Quite unaware of the thunder-cloud hanging
over his head, Colonel Delacombe came as usual,
and was sorry to hear of her ladyship's illness, but
any uneasiness he might have felt was dispelled
by May, who told him that Myrtilla was only
suffering from fatigue, and would be perfectly re-

stored after a few hours' rest. Satisfied with this assurance, he gave himself no further concern, but proceeded to his club.

Next morning, when he again presented himself in Eaton-place, he learnt that her ladyship was better, and was at once shown to her boudoir. He could not perceive any traces of illness in her countenance, but, on the contrary, thought her looking remarkably well, and told her so. She was writing a letter, and begged him to excuse her for a moment while she finished it. This gave her time to arrange her ideas.

When she addressed him, he saw in a moment that something was wrong. She did not waste time in any preliminary remarks, but said,

"In consequence of a communication made to me yesterday by Mrs. Sutton—the nature of which you will easily guess—I had resolved not to see you again, but to leave Sir Charles to acquaint you with my determination, together with my reasons for it, but ——"

"I am exceedingly glad you did not do so, Myrtilla," he interrupted. "What has Mrs. Sutton told you?"

Myrtilla hesitated, and the colour fled from her cheeks.

"If what she says is true, you have no right to pay your addresses to me or to any other lady. She affirms that you are already married. Can you give me your word of honour that there is no truth whatever in her statement?"

"No," he replied in a sombre tone, "I cannot do that."

"Then you admit the charge?"

"Certainly not."

"How am I to reconcile these contradictions?"

"Listen to me, Myrtilla. The disclosure I am about to make has been delayed too long—but on my honour I intended to make it. How the secret, which I thought confined to my own breast, has come to Mrs. Sutton's knowledge I do not pretend to guess. It is certain that she has learnt it, and now uses it for her own vindictive purposes. I will be as brief in my narration as I can, and I beg you not to interrupt me. When I first entered the army, and had little or no experience of your sex, I was entrapped into a marriage with an artful woman. I do not attempt to extenuate my conduct. All the reproaches you could heap upon me would not equal the reproaches I have heaped upon myself. I was mad—that is my sole excuse. I soon discovered how completely I had been duped. The perfidious wretch, with whom I had unfortunately connected myself, did not love me — did not even respect my honour. She had basely deceived me. Before I married her, she had a lover — and ere long, as I subsequently

ascertained, she renewed her intimacy with him,
if she had ever discontinued it. These particulars
must shock you, but I cannot withhold them.
They are necessary for my justification. The
woman's temper was frightful. At times she was
a perfect fiend — a terror to her mother, with
whom she lived — and I confess that I myself
was afraid of her, for, in her transports of fury,
my life was not safe. Upon one occasion, indeed,
she snatched up a knife, and would have stabbed
me if I had not wrested the weapon from her.
It is scarcely necessary to say that the degrading
alliance I had formed was kept secret. It was
not even known to my intimates. However, I
was not troubled with her long. When I went
to Ireland with my regiment, I left her with her
mother. She expressed no desire to accompany
me — probably, for the reasons I have already
given. I had no correspondence with her, and

heard nothing of her for months. I then only learnt her fate from a newspaper."

" What was her fate ?" demanded Myrtilla, who had listened with deep interest to his recital.

" She was drowned with her paramour while crossing the Severn during a gale. The ferry-boat was upset, and all on board perished. Justice overtook her. She had deserted her mother, whose heart was broken by her misconduct, and who died soon afterwards. Can you wonder that I should desire to bury such a deplorable history in oblivion ? Long years have passed since the events took place, but the recollection of them still gives me great pain."

" Was it clearly ascertained that the misguided woman perished ?"

" Undoubtedly. It was known that she and her lover embarked in the ferry-boat on that fatal night, and not a soul was saved."

There was a pause for some moments. At last, Myrtilla spoke:

"Seymour, I fear she still lives—lives to plague you in the form of Mrs. Sutton."

The colonel's brow darkened.

"I cannot hope to convince you," he rejoined, in a sombre tone. "Think what you please. But say no more on the subject."

"Do not be angry with me. Right or wrong, I will stand by you, and acting thus together, we shall prove more than a match for Mrs. Sutton."

"She can do me no injury except through you, Myrtilla. She is in my power, and if she provokes me further she shall feel that she is so."

"Take care you do not place yourself in *her* power, Seymour, or she will show you little pity. Marriage between us, under present circumstances, is of course out of the question; but I shall continue our friendly relations, if only to vex Mrs. Sutton. She shall not have the gratification of thinking she has produced a rupture."

" I swear to you, Myrtilla, you are mistaken——"

" Do not forswear yourself, Seymour. You will fail to convince me, unless you can prove that the Severn has not parted with its prey, which I think you will find rather difficult. But I will not give the vindictive woman a triumph. That is all I can promise you. One more question, and I have done. Answer it or not, as you please, but answer truly. Who is Hilary St. Ives?"

" Who is he?"

" Was there issue of your ill-starred marriage?"

The colonel made no reply.

" If there was, this young man is your son. I have thought so all along. Have you ever made any inquiries about him?"

" No. I take no interest in him. Even if

your suspicions are correct—and there is nothing
to warrant them—I will never acknowledge him.
It may seem a harsh determination—but having
formed it, I shall abide by it."

Just then the door opened, and Mrs. Radcliffe
came in, accompanied by May.

XVII.

A DISCUSSION UPON BALLS AND WHAT IT LED TO.

No one could have supposed from Mrs. Radcliffe's manner that she entertained any secret feeling of dislike to Myrtilla, or was otherwise than pleased at her recovery. Yet, if her heart had been searched, it would have appeared that she was vexed at seeing her rival look so well, and still more provoked to find her on as good terms as ever with the colonel. Naturally, she had attributed Myrtilla's sudden illness to the effect of Mrs. Sutton's communication. But if a quarrel had been caused, a reconciliation must have taken place, and consequently the mischief was undone.

Myrtilla discerned what was passing in the other's breast, and was malicious enough to heighten her annoyance.

Shortly afterwards, Sir Charles came in, and expressed his satisfaction at finding his sister all right again.

"You were terribly missed yesterday, Myrtilla, I can tell you," he said. "Your squires in Rotten-row were in despair at your non-appearance with May, and there was universal lamentation at the Opera. I did not go to Lady Louisa Legge's ball, but I hear it was considered a failure owing to your absence."

"Very flattering to us," remarked her ladyship, smiling. "We shall reappear with additional éclat at Mrs. Baldwin Lanyon's rout to-night. I insist upon your going with us, Charlie."

Sir Charles shook his head.

"No more balls for me," he remarked. "I am heartily sick of them. I went to bed early last night, and am all the better for it. You don't want me, May. I never dance, and you have no end of partners."

"Very well, sir, then we must do without you," cried Myrtilla. "But you will lose a very charming party. I dare say you would very much prefer a quiet evening at Boxgrove."

"Infinitely. I find no pleasure in crowded and stifling rooms, and there is nothing in the society one meets to compensate for the annoyance one is sure to experience."

"If such is your opinion, Charlie, you are quite out of place in a ball-room, and much better in bed," said her ladyship. "But to my mind there is nothing so delightful as a crowded ball— crowded I mean by nice people, such as we are sure to meet to-night at the Baldwin Lanyons'.

Whatever you may aver to the contrary, girls are never seen to such advantage as in a ball-room, and certainly there is no other kind of réunion that they enjoy so much. Isn't it true, May?"

The young lady appealed to made no reply. But Mrs. Radcliffe smiled assent.

"It used to be so in my time," she remarked.

"At no other sort of party can flirting be carried on to such an extent," observed Sir Charles, dryly; "and that I fancy is the grand recommendation of a ball."

"We all like to flirt a little at a ball or elsewhere," laughed Myrtilla; "and so do you in your quiet way, Charlie. Rail as much as you please against balls, young people will always enjoy them."

"To be sure they will," said Mrs. Radcliffe. "My health will not permit me to go out now;

but there was a time when I liked nothing so much as a ball."

"And were as much admired as your daughter, as I can bear witness," observed the colonel. "Sir Charles must be jesting. I never heard him advance such monstrous opinions before."

"You mistake my meaning," observed Sir Charles. "A ball now and then is delightful, but there may be too much of a good thing. To go out night after night—to meet the same crowds—to dance with the same triflers—to listen to the same vapid nonsense—appears to me a sad waste of existence."

This tirade was received with a loud burst of laughter from everybody but May.

"How we differ!" cried Myrtilla. "To me a ball looks like enchantment. I like the atmosphere and excitement, the lights, the music, the crowd, the talk, the dancing—everything."

" Especially the flirting," remarked her brother.

" Well, what do girls go to a ball for ; except to flirt, as you call it ? Most of them go with the expectation of finding husbands, and some of them succeed in their design. Necessarily, if they are pretty, they are admired, and men will flatter them—will talk nonsense to them. If they laugh and are amused, you call that flirting."

" But I hold it impossible that a girl of any sense can be amused by the frivolities and attentions of the same empty coxcombs," cried Sir Charles. " She may tolerate them for an occasion, but night after night to surround herself with the same set of idiots argues a very coquettish disposition."

" Well, then, I proclaim myself a coquette— a heartless coquette, if you please," cried Myrtilla. " I *do* like admiration — I *do* like to be sur-

rounded by a throng of empty-headed coxcombs,
vieing with each other for the honour of dancing
with me. It diverts me to listen to their nonsense,
and it enchants me to make them jealous of each
other. And I will tell you why, Charlie. A
man never looks so supremely ridiculous as when
he is jealous."

"None but a fool can be jealous of a coquette.
To be jealous of a woman you must love her, and
when you see her bestow her smiles on every one
who comes near her, the love you have felt will
soon be extinguished."

"There I differ with you," said the colonel.
"Our passions are not so much under our control
that we can conquer them in a moment. A coquette may vex and annoy us, but we cannot
cease to love her."

"Well, we have had a very long discussion
upon balls," remarked Myrtilla. "But, in spite

of all that Sir Charles has said, I shall go to
Mrs. Lanyon's rout to-night. How say you,
May?"

"You must excuse me," she rejoined.

"Why, surely you won't let Sir Charles's silly
opinions influence you?"

"I had made up my mind not to go before he
said a word—but I quite agree with him. I am
tired of balls."

"Are these your real sentiments, May?" cried
Sir Charles, in surprise.

"Myrtilla will tell you that it is not the first
time I have expressed them," she rejoined.

"Yes, since you are foolish enough to make
this confession, I must confirm its truth," replied
her ladyship. "I make no doubt it will gratify
you to learn, Charlie, that the silly creature,
finding you disliked balls, and were anything
but gratified—as you ought to have been—to see

her so much admired, and so much sought after,
would have withdrawn from society altogether,
if I would have allowed her. But I would not
hear of such a thing. I thought—and still think
—that you are bound to sacrifice your own
inclinations to her's, and that it is very selfish
of you to interfere with her enjoyment."

"But I have not found the enjoyment you led
me to expect in this perpetual round of gaiety,
Myrtilla," said May; "while, as you are aware,
the attentions paid me have been as annoying to
me as to Sir Charles. Forced to contrast my
former happy life with that I have been leading
of late, I am satisfied that my tastes are extremely simple—that the country suits me far
better than town—and that I am not at all cut
out to be a fine lady."

Sir Charles uttered a cry of delight.

"You are the most charming creature on earth,"

he exclaimed, flying towards her, and taking her hand, which he pressed to his heart, "and have dispelled every doubt I entertained."

"I know you thought me changed, dear Sir Charles," she said, regarding him affectionately; "but indeed—indeed—I am not so. I have played a foolish part, but if you knew how much I have suffered in acting it you would forgive me. I am still the same May as ever."

"Don't say any more, I beg of you, my love," cried Myrtilla. "You will totally spoil him. I hope he won't be so barbarous as to take you at your word."

"My desire is to return to Hazlemere immediately, if I am not interfering with mamma's plans," said May. "I shall ever feel obliged by your kindness to me, Myrtilla, but I have had enough of gaiety."

"Under the circumstances, I think you have

come to a very wise determination, my dear," remarked Mrs. Radcliffe. "You are bound to consult Sir Charles's wishes on all points. However,
you had better remain in town for a few days
longer, as your sudden departure might cause disagreeable comments."

"If I remain I shall not go to another ball.
People may say what they please."

"Well, I will make the best excuses I can for
you," remarked Myrtilla. "But I must keep *my*
engagements. What am I to say to Lord Robert,
and the rest of your admirers?"

"Bid them go hang themselves," cried Sir
Charles.

"They are very likely to do it when they hear
of May's departure," laughed the colonel. "You
will have a great deal to answer for, Sir Charles.
Society will not easily forgive you for depriving it
of its chief attraction."

"I am too happy to care what it thinks," cried the other, pressing May's hand.

That very morning May removed from Eaton-place to Upper Brook-street.

Thenceforward, she and Sir Charles were almost as much together as they had previously been in the country, and she declared with perfect sincerity that her last three days in town were the pleasantest she had spent there. There was plenty to do, for as the wedding-day was not far off, the trousseau had to be ordered, and other necessary arrangements made. These afforded delightful occupation to Mrs. Radcliffe, who liked nothing so much as a consultation with a modiste. It may interest our fair readers to learn that May received a profusion of handsome presents. Every day brought her a beautiful piece of jewellery. A new chariot had been ordered, and after she had inspected it, it was sent down to Boxgrove.

Thither Sir Charles prepared to follow, while the others got ready for their return to Hazlemere.

Their last day in town was devoted to the Crystal Palace, where grandpapa gave a capital dinner, as will be learnt in the next chapter.

XVIII.

AT THE CRYSTAL PALACE.

AFTER all, there is no place near London more enjoyable than the Crystal Palace. We cannot for a moment compare the gardens and grounds with those of the regal palace of Versailles. There is no grandeur about the enormous conservatory crowning Sydenham Hill, but it has a light and cheerful aspect, which a more solid structure in such a situation, and built with a similar object, could not offer. Its terraces, though wide, are not stately—but they do very well for a promenade.

Its lawns, which are its prettiest feature, are smooth and well kept, but then you are not allowed to walk upon them. It has abundance of shrubberies, plantations, flower-beds, and pavilions; it has many statues in plaster, which we do not admire, and it commands a magnificent and extensive view which every one *must* admire, when it is not obscured by fog; but it has no charming parterres like those of Versailles—no bosquets—no long shady alleys—no quincunxes—no tapis vert—no basin of Latona—no salle de bal—and above all, no fountain of Neptune.

Still, its fountains, though wanting in the rich sculpture of those of Versailles, answer their purpose, and when in full play present a very striking spectacle.

What with its various attractions, inside and out, the Crystal Palace constitutes, as we have said, the best place of amusement to be found near

the metropolis. Naturally, it is the favourite resort of foreigners, who find in the beautiful
gardens and in the vast bazaar connected with
them, more to suit their tastes than anywhere else
in London. Where are there such fêtes as those
of Sydenham? — where such concerts? — where
such fireworks? The glories of extinct Vauxhall
pale before the modern pyrotechnic displays, and
their wonderful accompaniments. Nothing can be
finer than the illuminated fountains.

But it is not our purpose to particularise the
numerous and varied attractions of the Crystal
Palace. We are not about to describe its courts
and galleries. All our readers must be familiar
with them. Everybody, however, may not know
how well you can dine there. We do not speak
of the general refreshment-rooms, of which we
know nothing; but we refer to the private dining-
rooms, where you can get a far better dinner and

far better wines, than at the renowned Hôtel des
Reservoirs at Versailles—and that is saying a good
deal.

Of this fact our worthy friend Mr. Thornton
had been made aware. The old gentleman had
already entertained the family party at Richmond
and Greenwich, and had got a capital dinner at
either place, but as the Radcliffes' visit to town
was drawing to a close, he resolved to wind up
with a dinner at the Crystal Palace, which, if
possible, should surpass the others. Accordingly
he secured a room and held a consultation with
the representative of Messrs. Bertram and Ro-
berts, who promised to carry out his intentions
efficiently, and to give him a most recherché
dinner—whitebait and fish as good as he had
eaten at Greenwich, and other delicacies superior
to those provided for him at Richmond. And
we may add that he kept his word.

There was a floral fête that day at the Crystal Palace, and as the show of roses was expected to be magnificent, all the party—with one exception—went early to see it.

The exception was Lady Richborough. She did not care for roses, and preferred starting at a later hour. The colonel would fain have tarried for her, but she declined his attendance, and he went on with the others.

Ever since the explanation, though her ladyship continued ostensibly on the same terms with him as before, she contrived never to be alone with him.

As ill luck would have it, at the Victoria Station she encountered Sir Charles's two pests, Lord Robert Tadcaster and Captain de Vesci, and though their company was agreeable enough in the train, she contrived to get rid of them on her arrival at the Palace, and proceeded alone through the grounds towards the central entrance. She had not gone far when a young man who was passing raised his hat to her. It was Hilary St. Ives, and she stopped him.

"I had determined to speak to you, Mr. St. Ives, if I should ever meet you," she said. "Will you take the trouble to walk a few steps with me?"

Hilary was delighted to obey.

"Your ladyship does me great honour," he observed. "I thought you had forgotten all about me."

"No, I have really something important to say to you. But first let me tell you that you have very much offended Miss Radcliffe."

"Indeed! I am very sorry to hear it. In what way have I offended her?"

"By sending the gipsy to her at Ascot. The jest may have afforded you amusement, but you ought to have considered that Miss Radcliffe was likely to be annoyed by it."

"I am sorry your ladyship should think me capable of doing anything in such excessively bad taste," cried Hilary, reddening. "The gipsy was *not* sent by me, neither have I the slightest notion what she said. I certainly observed her leaning over the side of the carriage, and whispering something in Miss Radcliffe's ear, but that is all I know of the matter. I was a mere accidental spectator of the scene. Pray tell Miss Radcliffe so. I would not for worlds give her annoyance."

"I will tell her exactly what you say," replied Myrtilla. "She will be glad to receive the assurance. Her marriage with my brother, Sir Charles Ilminster, is about to take place almost immediately."

"I wish them all happiness. Sir Charles will have a lovely bride. He is singularly fortunate in his choice. Miss Radcliffe is one in a thousand."

"You speak enthusiastically," rejoined her ladyship, smiling.

"I utter my real sentiments. Your ladyship's condescension emboldens me to ask a favour of you. Mrs. Radcliffe has expressed some interest in me. Will you kindly inform her that I am about to proceed immediately to Paris? I think I shall do better there than in London."

"I will convey the message," she rejoined. "But I hope I am not to understand from it that you have been unsuccessful in your profession as an artist? Can I be of any service to you?" she continued, with an expression of real interest. "I do not make the offer lightly. Some circumstances connected with your history have recently come to my knowledge, and have shown me that you have been badly treated. I have it in my power to help you, and I will do so, if you choose to assert your rights."

"Alas! I have no *rights* to assert. Your ladyship does not understand my unfortunate position."

"I understand it better than you suppose. Your position is *not* unfortunate, and can be easily remedied."

"Alas! not so. There is no redress for me. I cannot move without injury to one who has the chief claim upon my affections."

"She deserves no consideration. She is the sole obstacle to your recognition. Disregard her altogether."

"Not for worlds could I act thus. Reproach shall never touch her if I can prevent it. If your ladyship has obtained possession of the secret, I implore you to guard it strictly. Reflect, I beseech you, on the consequences of the slightest imprudence in a case involving the honour and happiness of so many persons. For the sake of those connected with her, I beseech your ladyship to spare her, and keep her secret."

"What mean you?" cried Myrtilla, amazed. "Why should I spare her? What is she to me? Your observations seem to apply rather to Mrs. Radcliffe than to Mrs. Sutton."

Hilary saw the error into which he had been led, and endeavoured to rectify it.

"I am so troubled that I scarcely know what I say," he rejoined. "But Mrs. Radcliffe is the last person to whom my observations could apply."

"They could not possibly refer to Mrs. Sutton," remarked Myrtilla.

"They were not intended to refer to her."

"To whom, then, did you allude?"

He tried to evade the question, and muttered something as her ladyship walked on slowly.

"You have perplexed me very much, Mr. St. Ives," she observed, after a short pause. "You have started a difficulty that I did not at all foresee. I think you are wrong, but be this as it may, you need fear no indiscretion on my part. I am not a mischief-maker. My sole desire is to see you righted, for I think you have been very badly used; but if this cannot be accomplished without detriment to others, I shall abandon the idea—at all events, for the present. I wish, however—if not inconvenient to yourself — that you would postpone your departure for Paris for a few days, and in the interim call upon me in Eaton-place. I should like to talk the matter over with you quietly."

Hilary promised compliance, and professing himself deeply indebted to her ladyship for the kind interest she had manifested in him, bowed and took leave.

Had the interview been prolonged, even for a

few minutes, it would have been disagreeably interrupted, for shortly afterwards Mrs. Radcliffe and the rest of the party appeared on the terrace, where Lady Richborough joined them.

Later on in the day—when an opportunity offered—she informed Mrs. Radcliffe of her meeting with Hilary, and delivered his message to her—carefully noting its effect.

Mrs. Radcliffe appeared much concerned. She had lost none of the interest with which the young man had originally inspired her.

" The news afflicts me greatly," she said. " He has immense talent as an artist, but merit is not properly appreciated. He seems very soon discouraged. I dare not say more to Colonel Delacombe about him, but a word from your ladyship would do wonders."

"I have offered my services to the young man, but he declines them."

" Poor fellow! he allows his pride to stand in

his way. A thousand pities that he is so impracticable. Pray speak to the colonel. He will listen to you, though not to me. If the young man is going to Paris immediately, no time must be lost. I will acquaint Sutton with his intended departure. She feels for him like a mother, as I do myself."

"By-the-by, have you ever found out who is his mother?"

"No. I have no curiosity on the subject. There is no doubt she is dead."

"I am not so sure of that," rejoined Myrtilla, looking at her.

"What reason has your ladyship for thinking otherwise?" cried Mrs. Radcliffe, surprised.

"I will tell you some other time. I cannot enter into particulars now."

"Can she be his mother?" she reflected.

This was May's first visit to the Crystal Palace,

and everything conspired to render it agreeable.
Sir Charles was with her, and his looks pro-
claimed his happiness. Others of the party were
equally delighted with the scene, for it had the
same charm of novelty to Mr. and Mrs. Radcliffe as to their daughter. The weather was
superb—bright and breezy. The numerous as-
semblage attracted by the flower-show completely
filled the interior of the building, which presented
a magnificent coup d'œil.

Out of doors the scene was equally attrac-
tive—more so, perhaps. As the company began
to stream forth and disperse among the grounds,
which were then in their fullest beauty, the
picture, as viewed from the terrace, was really
enchanting, and May and Sir Charles gazed at
it with delight.

As they were thus occupied in surveying the
charming prospect, interchanging their senti-

ments, and almost betraying their innermost emotions by their looks, they were watched from a distance by Hilary.

After taking leave of Lady Richborough, as related, the young man did not quit the palace, but contrived, though unobserved, to keep her ladyship in sight. He beheld her meeting with the party. He saw Mrs. Radcliffe and Colonel Delacombe—with what feelings need not be described Above all, he saw May.

Though his sentiments towards the latter were changed, he could not but regard her with the deepest interest, and he would have given worlds to exchange places with Sir Charles, and hold a brief converse with her.

He had much to say—much that never could be said—and it was not likely they should ever meet again. He might obtain a momentary glimpse of her—such as he now enjoyed—but that would be all.

How lovely she looked! How tender were the glances she bestowed on Sir Charles!—and how passionately devoted to her Sir Charles appeared. They were standing on the terrace, as we have described, too much occupied by the scene before them—too much engrossed by each other to re- mark that they were watched.

Near to them stood Colonel Delacombe, laugh- ing, and talking carelessly with Mrs. Radcliffe. Did either of them bestow a thought on *him*?

He turned from them to Lady Richborough, who was standing between Mr. Thornton and Mr. Radcliffe, and apparently delighting them both by her lively remarks. Her ladyship was evidently an object of general admiration, and Hilary could not help feeling flattered by the interest that had been taken in him by so charming a personage.

He still maintained his post of observation, when a ridiculous incident occurred that afforded a good deal of amusement to all who witnessed it.

The upper fountains had just begun to play, when two young men of very fashionable appearance, who had caught sight of Lady Richborough, and were hastening to join her, incautiously passed too near the jets, and were drenched from head to foot by the spray, which a sudden gust of wind carried over them.

Most pitiable objects they looked, with their dishevelled whiskers and dripping garments, and they hurried off as fast as they could to hide their discomfiture, but did not escape recognition as Lord Robert Tadcaster and Captain de Vesci. Mr. Radcliffe and Mr. Thornton laughed heartily, and Sir Charles was not sorry that such an example had been made of them.

An excellent dinner concluded a very agreeable day, so far as the majority of the party was concerned. Lady Richborough, however, had still something to do. She went to two balls that night.

Next day our friends left town—the Radcliffes and old Mr. Thornton for Hazlemere, and Sir Charles Ilminster for Boxgrove.

While bidding adieu to Mrs. Radcliffe, the colonel strongly urged her to get rid of Mrs. Sutton.

" I do not see how that can be managed, just at present," said the lady.

" She must go—and speedily—or she will make more mischief," rejoined the colonel.

Mrs. Radcliffe smiled. She thought the house-keeper had done all the mischief she could.

She was very much mistaken.

XIX.

LADY RICHBOROUGH RECEIVES A PROPOSAL.

It will naturally be imagined that Hilary would present himself without delay in Eaton-place. Three days passed by, however, and he had neither called nor sent an excuse.

Lady Richborough, who had begun to take a strong interest in his fortunes, was very much surprised and annoyed by his unaccountable neglect.

On the morning of the fourth day after she had met him at the Crystal Palace she was alone in her elegantly-furnished drawing-room, wondering whether he would call, and prepared to take him to task if he did, when a valet entered, and announced—not the young gentleman who occupied her thoughts, but — Mr. Thornton.

Though secretly disappointed, she immediately rose from the fauteuil on which she was reclining, and welcomed her visitor with every demonstration of delight. Her ladyship, we may remark en passant, was attired in a robe of toile de l'Inde, with deep flounces, which suited her admirably.

" Good morning, dear Mr. Thornton," she cried, in her blandest accents. " Enchanted to see you. Just come up from Hazlemere, I suppose? How did you leave them all? — dear Miss Radcliffe—darling May—and dear excellent Mr. Radcliffe?"

"All much as usual," replied the old gentleman. "The ladies desired their love to you, of course. Sir Charles dined with us yesterday, and we all dine with him to-day. Your ladyship will laugh when I tell you that May declares she will never come to town again, unless Sir Charles particularly desires it, and he invariably answers that she shall do just as she likes. Well, I hope it will last; they promise to be the happiest pair under the sun."

"Yes, if happiness consists in a quiet, humdrum, country life, with no excitement beyond a stroll in the garden, a canter in the park, or a visit to the stables, they are likely to get on well enough. But that is not my notion of happiness, as you are aware, Mr. Thornton. I like town life—gaiety, and plenty of it."

"I think your ladyship is quite right," rejoined the old gentleman. "I begin to find the country rather dull myself. But of course I must remain at Hazlemere till the grand business is over. Apropos of the wedding, the bridesmaids are chosen, Jessie Brooke, the two Miss Milwards, Eva Dale, Gwendoline Clifford, Elfrida Butler, Lucy Fleming, and Selina Hardy, eight uncommonly pretty girls. Captain Huntley Blois is to be Sir Charles's best ·man. The marriage, of course, will take place at Wootton, and our worthy vicar, the Rev. Nisbet Jones, will perform the ceremony."

"Is the day fixed, Mr. Thornton? It was not when they left town."

"Yes, I believe it will be the 15th, but your ladyship will receive precise information from May. I understand they don't mean to go abroad, or make any lengthened tour, but return after a week's absence to Boxgrove, and spend the rest of the honeymoon at home."

"Just like Charlie! I wonder May will consent to such a stupid arrangement. They ought to go to Switzerland, or the Italian lakes. Bellagio, on the lake of Como, would be delightful, and take Paris on the way back."

"Delicious!" exclaimed the old gentleman, rapturously. "If I ever take another wedding trip, I'll follow your ladyship's advice and go to Como. By-the-by, I've something to say to you."

"Before you say it, let me ask you whether that young artist — you know whom I mean, Hilary St. Ives—has been lately at Hazlemere?"

"Odd, you should ask me the question. I believe he was there yesterday, but I didn't see him."

"I suppose Mrs. Radcliffe sent for him?"

"What for!" exclaimed the old gentleman, staring at her. "Why should she send for him?"

"It occurred to me that she might have done so—but never mind. What have you got to say to me?"

"Something that requires your best attention," he rejoined. "I must premise that I am tolerably well off. Prudence and economy in early life—together with some fortunate speculations—have enabled me to realise a considerable property."

Myrtilla smiled. She suspected from his manner what was coming.

"I have always understood, Mr. Thornton, that you are rich—very rich," she observed.

"Not *very* rich, but rich enough to make a good settlement, as I am prepared to do, if your ladyship——"

"Really, Mr. Thornton, you take me quite by surprise," she cried, with difficulty repressing a laugh.

"I fear I have been too abrupt, but your ladyship will excuse me. Yesterday I learnt, for the first time, from my daughter, Mrs. Radcliffe, that all was at an end between your ladyship and Colonel Delacombe. I presume she was correctly informed?"

"No positive engagement ever subsisted between the colonel and myself, Mr. Thornton, and I may add none is likely to occur, but we are just as good friends as ever."

"Exactly. I understand. Comes to the same thing. Engagement, or no engagement, it's off."

"If you like to have it so—yes. And certain not to be renewed."

"Delighted to hear it—that is, sorry for my friend the colonel, for whom I have the greatest regard, but glad on my own account. Finding there was an opening for another suitor, I resolved to be first in the field, and here I am——"

"A word, Mr. Thornton. Pray did you acquaint Mrs. Radcliffe with your intention?"

"Most certainly, and Radcliffe too. I thought it only right and proper to consult them. They both highly approved of my design."

"Indeed! I should scarcely have expected it."

"They thought the match very desirable, as it would connect the families still more closely, and Sir Charles was of the same opinion. May was particularly well pleased. She thought it would be such a nice thing——"

"To have me for a grandmamma!" cried Myrtilla, laughing. "Excessively obliged to her."

"To have you for a grandmamma!" exclaimed Mr. Thornton, aghast. "Who ever dreamed of such a thing? You must think me crazy."

"You told me, only this moment, that you were resolved to be first in the field—what does that mean?"

"It means that I have come to make you an offer of marriage—not from myself—I have not the presumption—but from my grandson, Oswald Woodcot. Having been partly refused on a former occasion, the poor fellow has not the courage to present himself again, so I have undertaken to plead his cause; and perhaps I may be able to use some arguments that may have weight, if you will deign to listen to them."

"I will listen to anything you may say to me, Mr. Thornton, but I cannot understand why Oswald should require your intervention. I did not think bashfulness was his foible. Rather the reverse——"

"Well, if the truth must be told, he is without—anxiously, most anxiously, awaiting your decision. Shall I call him in?"

"By all means," she replied. "I am concerned that he should have been kept there so long."

Thereupon, the old gentleman opened the door, and his grandson immediately rushed in, and, flying towards her ladyship, threw himself in a theatrical manner at her feet. But she at once ordered him to rise.

"Such absurdity as this is out of date," she cried. "Nobody kneels now-a-days—except upon the stage. Do you know what you have done, sir? By your ridiculous mode of proceeding you very nearly made me accept Mr. Thornton."

"My stars! if I had known that, I would have gone in on my own account," cried the old gentleman. "You see what powers of persuasion I possess, Oswald."

"It appears to me that you have said one word for me and two for yourself, sir," observed his grandson, reproachfully.

"Don't be angry, my boy. All will be right in the end. The mistake will easily be rectified.

Take him on my recommendation," he said to Myrtilla. "I'll answer for it, he'll make an excellent husband."

" Have you told her ladyship what you propose to do, sir?"

"No; but I'll tell her now in your presence. What I promise I'll perform. If your ladyship accepts the proposal which I have just had the honour to make on behalf of my grandson, I undertake that a jointure shall be settled on you corresponding in amount with that which you now enjoy, and which you will lose on your marriage."

" Upon my word, you do the thing very handsomely, I must say, Mr. Thornton," she observed, smiling.

" But that's not all," cried Oswald. " My dear old grand-dad is the most liberal fellow on earth."

" So he seems," she assented.

"I always intended to make Oswald my heir," pursued the old gentleman. "But if he marries to please me—as he will, if he marries your ladyship—he shall have a handsome allowance during my lifetime."

"Didn't I say he was a capital fellow?" cried Oswald.

"My desire is to make all pleasant," added the old gentleman; "and I hope I shall be able to go back to Hazlemere and tell them that the affair is satisfactorily settled."

"Now for the decision," said Oswald. "My happiness and my fortune rest with your ladyship."

"I must have time for consideration," she rejoined. "I should like to please Mr. Thornton, who has behaved so remarkably well, and to whom I feel personally indebted, and I have no particular objection to you, Oswald, but I can't make up my mind at a moment's notice."

"Then I am neither accepted nor rejected?" said the young man, looking very blank.

"Can't I prevail on your ladyship to say 'Yes'?" insinuated the old gentleman.

She shook her head, and rejoined, "Neither you nor Oswald understand me in the least. You have to do with the most fickle creature on earth. Were I to give you a promise now, ten to one I should break it, and then you would upbraid me with falsehood, inconstancy, and all that sort of thing. Don't press me further. I repeat, I can't make up my mind."

"Well, I still hope your ladyship may spend a month at the lovely lake of Como, and that I may have the pleasure of meeting you at Paris when you return."

"Not this autumn, I think, Mr. Thornton," she rejoined.

"We shall see—we shall see."

Just then, the valet entered, and approaching ·
Myrtilla, said:

" Mr. Hilary St. Ives is here. Will your ladyship see him ?"

She coloured slightly, as she answered in the
affirmative.

" What the deuce is he doing here ?" cried Mr.
Thornton.

" Come to take her ladyship's portrait, of
course," remarked Oswald.

" He has called by my express invitation," observed Lady Richborough. " Pray don't run
away on his account. Luncheon will be ready
directly. Do me the favour to step down to the
dining-room; I'll join you as soon as my con-
ference with Mr. St. Ives is ended."

The proposition was too agreeable to be declined. As the two gentlemen were quitting the
room, Hilary was ushered in, and they met near

the door. Mr. Thornton bowed very stiffly, but Oswald gave the young artist a good-natured nod of recognition.

" I don't know how it is," remarked Oswald to his grandsire, as they went down-stairs; "but that confounded fellow seems always to cross my path."

XX.

IN WHICH HILARY FINDS A FATHER.

"You have made very little haste to call upon me, Mr. St. Ives," observed Lady Richborough, motioning him to take a seat. "However, I do not require any apologies. I have just learnt from Mr. Thornton that you have been at Hazlemere."

"I was summoned there," he replied. "On the morning after I was fortunate enough to meet your ladyship at the Crystal Palace, I received a letter from Mrs. Radcliffe enjoining me

to come down to her without delay, and could not
refuse compliance, though I had resolved never
to go to Hazlemere again.   In obedience to the
instructions given me, I went down by a particular train.   Mrs. Sutton met me at the station
and conducted me to the house.   I had an interview with Mrs. Radcliffe, which I need not detail,
except to say that I consented to act according to
her directions."

"You did well," observed Myrtilla.   "I am
certain she would advise you for the best."

"I felt so," he replied; "and though stung
by a sense of injustice which prompted a very
different course, I yielded to her entreaties, and
agreed not to depart for Paris without seeing
Colonel Delacombe.   Mrs. Radcliffe assured me
—as I cannot doubt—that no one has so much
influence with the colonel as your ladyship—and
she assured me also that you are willing to exert
it in my behalf."

"My influence with Colonel Delacombe is not so great as Mrs. Radcliffe imagines," replied Myrtilla; "but I should like to hear something more about Mrs. Sutton. Had you no conversation with her? Had she no suggestions to offer?"

"Mrs. Sutton's manner towards me is incomprehensible," he rejoined. "Nothing could exceed the delight that she exhibited when she met me at the station. If I had been really her son, she could not have greeted me with more affection. But before we reached the house her manner had totally changed. Perhaps I did not please her by my observations, for she seemed to resent them. I am certain that she dislikes—I might almost say hates — Mrs. Radcliffe ; and she entertains no more kindly feeling towards Colonel Delacombe. She gives me the idea of a person in possession of an important secret which she uses for her own purposes."

"It is a great misfortune that she is installed at Hazlemere, and I fear Mrs. Radcliffe will have reason to regret the trust she places in her. If Mrs. Sutton were not in the way, I should have no difficulty with Colonel Delacombe. Do not ask me for any explanation. I cannot give it. Was she present during your interview with Mrs. Radcliffe ?"

"No; and I was very cautious in what I said to her, for, in spite of her professions of regard, her manner inspired me with distrust. I ought to mention that Mrs. Radcliffe told me she would write to the colonel, and beg him to confer with your ladyship. A few days ago I should not have cared to succeed, but now I ardently desire to do so."

"What has produced this sudden change in your sentiments?" she inquired.

"I am ambitious," he cried. "I have aspira-

tions which I ought not to indulge, but which
I cannot help indulging. At all hazards I must
speak the truth. Ever since our meeting, your
image has haunted me, and will not be dismissed. I am an artist, and you will not wonder
that beauty, such as yours, should produce an
extraordinary effect upon me. I tried to control
the passion inspired by your charms, but it has
mastered me. Never has my position appeared
so intolerable as now. I would be something
better—something on which you would not dis-
dain to cast your regards. I know you will laugh
at my folly and extravagance, but at least you
will understand why I desire to attain a higher
position."

Lady Richborough did not appear offended.

"If I have any rights, as you intimated when
we last met, I am resolved to assert them," he
pursued.

"The best thing to cure you of your romantic folly would be to allow you to remain as you are," she observed. "But I have promised to aid you, and I will be as good as my word. Pray did you make Mrs. Radcliffe a confidante of your passion?"

The young man looked abashed.

"She may have drawn her own conclusions from the raptures in which I spoke of your lady-ship's charms," he said.

"I thought as much," she rejoined. "That accounts for a visit I have just received."

An interruption here occurred. Colonel Dela-combe was ushered in by the valet, who imme-diately retired.

Hilary at once arose and prepared to depart, but Lady Richborough detained him.

Then turning to the colonel, who did not mani-fest either surprise or displeasure on seeing the young man, she said,

"I am very glad you have come, colonel. Mr. St. Ives has just laid his case before me, and I have undertaken to become his advocate."

"He could not have a better," rejoined the other. "It may save time, however, if I state at once that my mind is made up. This morning I have received a long letter from Mrs. Radcliffe. She, too, is a zealous advocate in the young man's cause, and pleads it warmly and strongly. But her pleading, I confess, would have been of no avail but for a wholly unforeseen circumstance. Doubts have rested on my mind that have warped my judgment and feelings, and converted what should have been affection into hate. These doubts have just been removed. How, or by whom, I need not now explain, but proofs have been afforded me that I was utterly wrong in my suspicions. Satisfied of this, 1 could not for a moment hesitate to repair the injustice I have done. Learning that the young man was here, I came on instantly. In your ladyship's presence, I acknowledge him as my son."

Hilary uttered an exclamation of joy, and threw himself into his father's outstretched arms.

"Nobly done, Seymour," cried Myrtilla. "You have not belied my expectations."

"I cannot suitably express my feelings of gratitude," said Hilary, in accents broken by emotion. "But this moment makes amends for all the past."

"Let the past be forgotten," said the colonel. "You will not blame me too severely when you know all. I will endeavour to atone for the error I have committed."

"Enough, sir—more than enough," cried his son.

"I cannot obey the dictates of my heart, which prompt me at once to acknowledge you publicly," said the colonel. "For some little time longer you must be content to remain Hilary St. Ives. But you need give yourself no concern in regard to the future. Henceforward, your position is completely assured."

"I beg to offer you my sincere congratulations, Mr. St. Ives, for I suppose I must still call you so," said Lady Richborough, archly. "You have now obtained the position you so much desired."

The colonel detected the glance that passed between her ladyship and the young man.

"His position and his fortune—for he will have both," he observed, in a significant tone—"will enable him to marry well."

"You mean to leave him behind, when you return to India, colonel?" she inquired.

"That depends," he replied. "If he should be fortunate enough to marry, his wife may not object to go out with us. I think I have heard your ladyship say that you would like to visit the country."

" Yes, I have said so, but I never meant it seriously."

" For my own part I have the greatest desire to visit India," cried Hilary. " It has every sort of attraction for me."

"You expect great things, I perceive; but I don't think you will be disappointed," said the colonel. " You will find plenty of employment there for your pencil, if you choose to exercise it."

" And plenty of charming society, I suppose ?" observed Hilary.

"The pleasantest society on earth—especially to ladies," rejoined the colonel. " Nowhere, as I have often remarked to Lady Richborough, are ladies made so much of as in India. A

beautiful woman is positively adored there, and
exercises a sway quite unattainable in England."

"A tempting description," observed Hilary,
glancing at her ladyship.

"Perhaps I may go to India, when I have
nothing better to do," she remarked, with a smile.
"But come down to luncheon. It must be ready.
Some of our friends from Hazlemere are here,"
she added to the colonel.

Upon this they descended to the dining-room,
where they found Mr. Thornton and Oswald,
both of whom were very glad to see the colonel,
but amazed that Hilary had not departed. An
elegant collation was speedily served, and a glass
of champagne raised Oswald's spirits. He would
have felt far happier, however, if her ladyship
had not paid so much attention to Hilary. Neither he nor his grandsire could understand the
remarkable change in Colonel Delacombe's de-

portment towards the young artist. He now treated him with so much friendliness that the old gentleman whispered to Oswald :

"Begad! it wouldn't surprise me if he were to acknowledge him, after all."

This impression was confirmed by a remark made by the colonel to Lady Richborough, seeming to imply that Hilary was going with him to his hotel.

Indeed, there could be no doubt on the point, since Mr. Thornton, being curious enough to look out of the dining-room window, beheld Hilary jump into the brougham, which was drawn up at the door, and heard the order given by the colonel to drive to the Langham.

Prior to his departure, the colonel had charged the old gentleman with a message to Mrs. Radcliffe to the effect that he meant to run down to Hazlemere on the following day. But he didn't add—as Mr. Thornton half expected—that he meant to bring Hilary with him.

Grandsire and grandson lingered for a few minutes in the vain hope of obtaining some encouragement from Lady Richborough. Her ladyship, however, did not relent.

END OF VOL. II.

LONDON :

C. WHITING, BEAUFORT HOUSE, DUKE STREET, LINCOLN'S-INN-FIELDS.